THE RED DUN FILLY

1265-CLEM

THE RED DUN FILLY

Bonnie Clement

1265-CLEM

To order additional copies of this book, contact:
Xlibris Corporation
1-888-7-XLIBRIS
www.Xlibris.com
Orders@Xlibris.com

CONTENTS

CHAPTER ONE:
"KLONK!"

Melody snatched her arm back inside the car and rubbed the spot scorched by the metal. The wind rushing past her face, though far from being cool, was a welcome relief from the still heat in town. The roar of air past her ears, along with the Geo's squeaks and groans, made holding a conversation with her mother practically impossible. Melody silently gazed out the window and across the wide, bowl-like valley. She hadn't fully believed her parents when they first told her their new home was going to be in an area much like her beloved Montana. As the landscape unfolded before her, however, Melody had no trouble seeing the similarities between the two places.

Montana. A twinge of homesickness made her eyes mist slightly. Had it really been seven years since they left her birth home for the noise and crowds of Seattle? That was over half a lifetime away, yet Melody could still vividly remember her first home along the banks of a spring-fed stream where she had better luck catching Mom's chickens with worm-baited hooks than she did the elusive trout. And there were the goats. When she was only three, Melody had learned how to milk on the patient, mostly white Alpine-Nubian goat named Judy. And there was Bouncer, a black-and-white kid who had lived up to his name and who had been adept at climbing the huge leaning willows along the stream. She hoped they had been happy in their new home and that Bouncer hadn't ended up in somebody's freezer as most of the male goats in each year's kid crop did. Melody had eaten a lot of goat meat her first six and a half years—most people couldn't tell it from extra lean beef once Mom finished cooking it—but Bouncer had been special; he had been her pet.

The pungent odor of skunk filled the car. Melody had actually missed that smell in Seattle. The stench of diesel and hot asphalt had been far more objectionable to her nose than skunk spray's sharp, acrid aroma. The road wound between two hills and past a field full of purple-blossomed alfalfa. The sweet scented flowers chased away the last residue of skunk. Melody breathed deeply. She loved the smell of alfalfa in bloom. She knew the farmer would soon be cutting that field for hay. She remembered their landlord in Montana and how he would let her ride with him on the tractor while he cut the field next to their mobile home—that was, whenever Jeff and Randy, her brothers, weren't around and got to ask him first. She loved her brothers, but she was also glad they were old enough now to live away from home. Because they were so much older than she was, they always felt they had the right to boss her around.

Mrs. Morrison turned off the paved road and on to a graveled road marked with a sign, "Primitive Road—No Warning Signs." It was primitive all right, Melody thought, as they hit a section ridged like the inner layer of corrugated cardboard. She wondered when was the last time it had been graded. Probably not since spring thaws three or four months ago was her guess.

"How soon before we get there?" Melody asked. The road seemed to go on for miles, and the broken spring in the seat was poking her in a very uncomfortable place.

"We should be coming up to the cattle guard soon," her mother replied. "After we cross that, it's only about a half mile farther."

Melody sighed and settled back against the car seat. The glare from the sun was giving her a headache, and her shirt was sticking to her back. Besides, she had been sitting in one spot long enough.

"There's the cattle guard!" She shouted and pointed ahead to slanted wooden posts on either side of the road. Several metal bars like train rails spaced several inches apart from each other spanned the space between the posts. Melody knew cattle wouldn't, as a rule, cross such a grating.

The little car lurched as Mrs. Morrison turned on to a rutted, one-track lane. "Looks as if they might have a bit of trouble in mud season," she commented while wrestling with the steering wheel.

"No different than Montana," Melody said. "Remember when Jo sank up to her axles in our driveway?"

"And with four-wheel drive, too! I don't know what was more covered in mud, us or the truck." Both of them laughed at the memory.

The lane twisted around a low hill, revealing a semi-circular, shallow pocket within the hills before them. The girl's eyes followed a wide sweep of tall grass dotted with grazing horses and cattle. The lane turned on to a shale-paved, roughly rectangular yard bordered on the south by a cottage that was more gray than white in spots and that was almost hidden by an overgrown border of mixed flowers. Melody recognized daisies, cosmos, snapdragons and delphiniums. Along the north side of the yard she noticed a long, low building, which she guessed was the stable. Several doors had the upper half open, and framed in each was a horse looking curiously in their direction. Melody wondered about the use of the large, open-sided roofed area at the far end of the yard.

Melody's hand was on the car door handle when a group of dogs rounded the corner of the barn. There were five of them, all black and white, or white and black, depending on the dominant color. All were barking in warning or in greeting—Melody didn't know which—but she wasn't about to test the intentions of so many at one time.

A short, stocky woman followed closely behind the dogs. Beneath the brim of the stained leather hat perched on short-cropped hair, a half smile crossed her face when she saw who they were. With one word, "Down!" all five dogs quieted, lying down in a loose group, tongues lolling and their eyes following every move their owner and the strangers to their territory made.

"Did you have any trouble finding us, Jen?" she asked Melody's mother once she came within speaking distance.

"Your directions were perfect," Mrs. Morrison said. "Melody, this is Abigail Jankins, the woman I work with at my job."

Melody look shyly at the woman's weather-seamed face. "Hi."

"Just call me Abby. Everyone else does." She held out a calloused hand.

Hesitating slightly, Melody took it. Abby's rough grip was a mixture of strength with an equal measure of gentleness.

Something tapped her leg below the knee. Looking down, Melody saw one of the dogs sitting by her and gazing up with soft brown eyes. His paw rested lightly on her jeans, and his partially open mouth made it look like he was grinning. She reached down and touched the silky black hair between tulip-shaped ears. A warm wet tongue licked her arm, and kept licking to get the dried salt on her skin.

"Oh, that's Mick," Abby said, stopping what she was saying to Melody's mother. "He's not much of a watchdog, but he sure knows how to welcome people. He'll keep you company, Mel, if you want to go over and see the horses."

The last word was barely out of the woman's mouth and Melody was sprinting toward the barn, Mick loping gleefully behind her. The other dogs started to follow, but lay back down at a word from Abby. Melody slowed to a walk as she approached the stalls. For as long as she could remember, she loved horses, but her actual experience with them had been limited. Her dream was to have a black horse like the ones she saw in movies like the Black Stallion or Black Beauty. When her father was offered a teaching job at the college in this farming community, she hoped her dream would finally come true. But a non-tenured professor didn't have money to spare, and her mother had been unable to find a full-time job. There was no way they could afford to buy a horse for her. No, her dream would have to wait a while. In the meantime, she could hope for riding lessons, but that depended on what arrangements her mother could make with Abby.

Melody stopped in front of a stall occupied by a golden colored horse with a reddish mane. A prehensile lip stretched toward her. Melody reached up to touch the velvety muzzle. Running her hand up between the eyes, she rubbed the broad forehead. An inverted white boot ran down the length of the horse's face. She laid her face against the sleek neck and breathed in the warm horsey smell.

"That's Dont Skippa Dance," Abby's voice said behind her. "We call her Dancer for short."

"She's beautiful! What kind of horse is she?"

"American Quarter Horse." Abby reached up and rubbed Dancer behind the ears. The horse leaned her head into her hand.

"Why does she have a name like Dont Skippa Dance?"

"That's her registered name. If you looked at her papers you'd see several of her ancestors with the name Skipper-something-or-other."

"How old is she?" Melody ran her hand through the unruly mane; the reddish hue nearly matched the color of her own hair.

"She's not quite two. I'm going to start training her this week."

"Is she a palomino?"

"No, she's what we call a red dun. See that stripe running along her backbone?'

Melody looked and nodded.

"That's called a dun-factor stripe. All dun horses have it. She's called a red dun because of the red mane and tail."

"Will she be one of the horses I'll get to ride?" Melody asked.

Abby chuckled. "No, dear, you'll take lessons on Miss Piggy down there." She pointed toward the end of the row.

Melody's expression fell when she saw the ewe-necked gray horse in the end stall.

"Oh, she's not a whole lot to look at," Abby said, "but she's got a lot of sense and knows how to take care of a green rider."

"Green rider?"

"Someone who knows little or nothing about horses. Just as we call an unbroke or barely broke horse a green horse."

"Oh." Melody gave Dancer's neck one more hug and turned to go down to see Miss Piggy.

There was a loud "klonk!" Sudden pain made Melody fall to her knees. She grabbed the top of her head where something heavy had hit it.

Her mother hurried to her side. "Are you okay?" she asked, helping the girl to her feet.

"I think so," Melody said, rubbing her head. "What happened?" She looked around into Dancer's large innocent eyes.

A smile tugged at Abby's mouth as she struggled to keep a straight face. "I'm afraid Dancer didn't want you to leave."

"What did she do? That hurt!"

"Well, she sorta dropped her jawbone on top of your head—at least that's what I think I saw out of the corner of my eye. I think she meant to put her head over your shoulder. She likes you."

"She has a funny way of showing it." Melody backed away several feet from Dancer's stall before turning to check out Miss Piggy.

CHAPTER TWO: MISS PIGGY AND DANCER

Melody watched Abby get Miss Piggy ready for her riding lesson. The sway-backed mare stood quietly while the woman lifted each foot and carefully cleaned out the mud and manure packed in the hollow of the hoof.

"Why do you do that?" Melody asked.

Without looking up, Abby replied, "Have you ever walked with sand or stones in your shoes?"

"Yes. It didn't feel very good."

"Well, that's why I do this."

"But wild horses don't get their feet cleaned," Melody said. "Don't their feet get clogged with dirt and stuff?"

"You'd think so, but wild horses don't wear shoes. See how the edge catches and holds the dirt and stuff in the hoof?" Abby dug out the accumulation with the hoof pick and showed Melody how the inner edge of the shoe overhung the inside wall of the hoof. She let Miss Piggy's foot down. "Besides, wild horses don't spend a lot of time standing in a stall or paddock and walking in their own poop all day. They get to run on hard and soft ground and wade in ponds and streams. All of that helps keep their feet cleaned, trimmed and hard."

Standing straight, Abby placed her hands behind her hips and stretched backwards. "I'm getting too old for this," she groaned. "Go into the tack room and bring me the saddle closest to the door, would you?"

"What's a tack room?" Melody asked.

Abby looked at her a moment, then she grinned. "It's that room down there." She pointed to the end of the row of stalls. "It's where the saddles, bridles and other horse equipment is kept."

"Oh," Melody said, and she hurried away to carry out Abby's request. *She must think I'm a real dork*, she thought, *but how was I to know what a tack room was? Boy, there's an awful lot to learn about horses.*

The tack room was dark and cool. Melody wanted to spend a few minutes in it, but she was here to ride. Her mother was doing some work on the ranch books for Abby in trade for the lesson. A scuffed-up saddle with a broad, flat horn sat on a rack mounted on the wall right inside the door. Hoping she knew what she was doing, Melody grasped the saddle in front of the horn and behind the cantle, as she had seen actors in movies do, and slid it off the rack. The sudden weight pulled her over and she landed in a heap over the top of the saddle. Melody picked herself up. With a great deal of effort, she managed to lift the saddle.

Staggering out to Abby and Miss Piggy, she dropped it on the ground. "How much does this thing weigh?" she gasped.

"About forty or fifty pounds." Abby picked the saddle up and swung it easily over the horse's back. "I have lighter ones, but this is the only one that fits Piggy comfortably." Reaching under the horse, Abby pulled the cinch to her side. She looped the leather end through rings fastened to the saddle and belly band several times, then pulled it tight until the saddle was fastened snugly on Miss Piggy. " Come on," Abby said, "up with you now."

Melody placed her left foot in the left stirrup and tried to pull herself up. Piggy wasn't a tall horse—at least not as tall as Dancer who was watching everything from her stall, but Melody found it hard to get the proper leverage with her leg.

"Once you're up, lean over the saddle to balance yourself," Abby instructed her. "Then swing your leg over."

Melody finally got her left leg straightened. She leaned over the saddle as Abby told her too, but too far. She nearly pitched off the other side. Abby caught her by the belt and pulled her upright. Melody swung her right leg across Miss Piggy's rump, brushing it with her foot. The horse flinched, but continued standing still. A moment later, Melody was mounted on a real horse, not just a pony, for the first time in her life. She sat with her back yardstick straight and her hands held high above the saddle horn. She tightened the muscles in her legs. Miss Piggy began walking forward.

"Wh-whoa!" Melody shouted, hauling back on the reins. Her legs gripped the saddle tighter.

Miss Piggy broke into a teeth-rattling trot.

"S-s-stop! W-whoa! Whoa!" Melody grabbed the saddle horn with both hands and tried to stay in the saddle while being bounced up and down.

Abby ran up and caught the nearer rein. Miss Piggy stopped suddenly, throwing Melody forward. She nearly flipped over the front of the saddle. As it was, she had to grab hold of the horse's neck to keep from falling off.

"What made her go like that?" Melody asked, sitting back up in the saddle. "I didn't kick her or anything."

"Then you must have squeezed her with your legs."

"I had to in order to stay on."

"Nope. You stay on by balancing yourself in the saddle and letting your body move with your horse. Relax. Stop sitting like you have a rod down your back. Let your back curl a little."

Leading Miss Piggy, Abby walked to a round sandy area enclosed with a fence constructed with steel panels coated with peeling orange paint. She let go of the rein and walked to the center of the ring.

"Relax your back."

Melody tried to loosen her back muscles, but years of practicing good posture were hard to overcome.

"Lower your hands. You're not some movie cowboy."

Melody dropped the level of her hands to waist height.

"Okay. That's good. Now squeeze gently with your legs."

Remembering what happened before, Melody barely tightened her legs against the horse's side. Nothing happened.

"A little harder."

This time Miss Piggy moved forward at a slow walk. For the next hour Abby instructed Melody how to use her hands and legs and body weight to guide the horse. The girl tried to master sitting more relaxed once Abby told her the stiff posture she had seen riders using in the movies wasn't practical for western style riding. There was so much to think about. At times she wondered if she would ever become a good rider.

Melody wasn't sure exactly how the memory surfaced, but she found herself thinking back to when she was a toddler. Her favorite toy had been Wonder Horse®, a molded plastic horse suspended on springs within a steel tubular frame. She would spend hours riding her "horsey." At times she would get so wild the frame would lift up off the floor and bounce across the room. To her embarrassment, Mom would tell friends that Melody wore out two Wonder Horses® before she was even out of diapers.

Why am I thinking about this? she wondered. *I was just a baby on a toy moving up and down and back and forth with the movement I made.* Suddenly she knew what she was doing wrong. As a baby she had moved with the toy. She didn't sit stiffly and let it jerk her around. Melody began to let her body move with Miss Piggy's motion. Immediately, she felt the difference. She and the horse were becoming synchronized.

"That's the way," Abby said. "You're getting it now. You've been at the walk quite a while now. Want to try the jog?"

"What's the jog?"

"Like the trot, only slower."

"Sure."

"Okay. Now Piggy is a bit rough, but try to just let yourself move with her. Squeeze your legs a little more and kiss to her."

Melody looked at Abby. "Kiss to her?"

"You know—make a sound like kissing."

"Oh." Melody's face reddened. *Abby must think I'm a real dummy,* she thought, *but I didn't know.*

Abby had understated Miss Piggy's roughness at the jog.

Melody felt like a sack of potatoes being jounced around. It was impossible to sit relaxed.

"That'll be enough for today," Abby said after a couple of minutes. She took hold of the reins while Melody dismounted. "Go ahead and unsaddle and brush Piggy before putting her in the stall. I'm going to begin working with Dancer."

Melody took the old gray mare back to the row of stalls and unsaddled her. She watched Abby take Dancer from her stall and lead her to the round pen. The sun glinted off the horse's reddish gold coat. Melody drew in her breath sharply. With her white legs and blaze, Dancer had to be the most elegant horse she had ever seen. Melody hurriedly brushed Miss Piggy and put her in the stall.

By the time Melody reached the round pen, Abby was having Dancer walk in different directions. There was no rope connecting them; the older woman was guiding the horse solely by the position of her body in the center of the pen. Abby made a kissing sound, and Dancer began jogging. Melody's mouth dropped open. She didn't know if it was the four white legs that created the illusion, or if Dancer hesitated slightly with each beat, but the horse seemed to float above the ground. The filly's stable name certainly fit her.

Abby saw Melody's expression. "Smooth, isn't she?"

"Did you train her to go like that?"

Abby laughed. "No. That's just her natural way. She's going to be a nice saddle horse for someone someday."

"Will I get to ride her sometime?"

Abby's smile diminished. "No, I don't think so," she said. "As soon as I have her trained to the saddle, I'm going to have to sell her."

"But, why?"

"I can't afford to keep every horse," Abby replied. "It costs too much to feed them, especially through the winter. And in order for me to keep the ranch, I have to be in the business of raising and selling horses."

"Could I buy her?" Melody asked.

A half smile touched Abby's mouth. "Ah, girl, you've got stars in your eyes. Right now you're ready to fall in love with any horse that you think might remotely be yours one day. My advice is for you to forget about Dancer. She probably costs more than your parents can afford in the first place. In the second place, she's a green, inexperienced horse and needs an experienced rider. You need an older, experienced horse that can teach you. Like Miss Piggy, for instance."

Melody grimaced. Miss Piggy was a sweet old horse, but far from her dreams of a dashing, elegant steed she could ride over the hills in search of adventure. No, Miss Piggy might be a good horse for her to learn how to ride on; but she wanted a horse like Dancer, a horse that would make heads turn when she rode by. True, Dancer wasn't black like her dream horse had been; but Melody didn't care. Dancer was simply the most beautiful horse she'd ever been this close to. Besides, the horse liked her. She proved that the first time they met.

Abby finished Dancer's lesson and snapped the lead to the halter.

"Can I put her away?" Melody asked.

Abby hesitated. "Well, I guess she'll be okay. You seem to have a way with animals." She handed the end of the lead rope to Melody. "Just remember, she's still a baby, so move slowly around her. And remember what I showed you when you brush her."

Melody reached up and petted Dancer's neck and ran her fingers through the unruly dark red mane. The filly leaned into her touch as if to say, "Scratch some more, please."

She took her time taking care of Dancer. She brushed the horse with long, slow strokes and took special care to give added attention to the areas where Dancer wanted extra scratching. One of those places was where the base of the tail met the rump. When Melody used the rubber curry there, Dancer would lean hard into her hand and would stretch out her neck and get a dreamy look in her eyes. Her upper lip would curl slightly. Melody laughed as the goofy expression came over the horse's face.

Melody could have spent the rest of the afternoon with the red dun, but she still had stalls to clean as part of her bargain to help pay for riding lessons. Reluctantly, she returned Dancer to her stall, closed the lower portion of the door and latched it. She hugged the horse's neck one more time and whispered, "I love you, Dancer. Somehow I've just got to make you mine." Dancer nuzzled her in agreement.

CHAPTER THREE: NEW KID

"There's no way we can afford a horse," Mr. Morrison said. "Besides, we have no place to keep it."

"We could arrange to make payments," Melody said. "Isn't that how you and Mom are buying the car and house?"

"We're at the limit of what we can afford in payments right now. As it is, your mother is already doing extra work just so you can have riding lessons." Mr. Morrison turned back to his computer, silently dismissing her. That signaled the end of the conversation as far as he was concerned.

He doesn't understand, Melody fumed. She stomped to her room and half slammed the door. Upset as she was, she maintained enough self control not to give full vent to her anger. Throwing herself on the bed, she let disappointment wash over her. *It isn't fair,* she thought. *Here they tell me we are moving to a perfect place for horses, and now Dad says we can't afford one. Period. No discussion. No trying to figure out how we can.*

There was a knock and the door opened slightly. "May I come in?" Mrs. Morrison asked.

Melody rolled over to her side. She sat up and nodded. With her fists she pressed tears out of her eyes as her mother closed the door and sat beside her on the bed.

"You'll have to forgive your father," she said. "Things are a little tight right now, and you know how he is about money."

"But he won't even take the time to see if there is any possible way," Melody protested.

"Give him time. Let him think about it. He may change

his mind later."

"Yeah. Right."

"Melody, you're not being fair. We've had a lot of expenses lately with your dad going to school and with moving out here for him to take the job at the university."

"Mom, do you think I'll ever be able to have a horse?"

"Maybe, in time. Horses are expensive to keep. They're not like a dog or cat."

"I could get a job and help pay for it," Melody said.

"There's not very many jobs a thirteen-year-old can do. A lot of places won't hire teens until they're sixteen or older."

"I could find something. I know I can."

Mrs. Morrison smiled. "Yes, I believe you could. In the meantime, pray about it. You never know. God very often gives us things we want when we put Him first. And remember, even if you do get a horse, your school work has to come first."

Melody made a face. School started in the morning, and she wasn't looking forward to it. Not only was she attending a new school in a new town, she had never attended a public school before. Both in Montana and in Seattle she had gone to Christian-run schools. Her brothers had related horror stories about public schools. She knew some of them must be true; otherwise, why had her dad so willingly paid the extra expense of private schools for her. True, the new school had only about four hundred students from kindergarten to twelfth; but even that number seemed awfully large after the small schools she attended.

Melody sighed. She missed her friends in Seattle; but when she thought about it, that was all she missed about living in the city. She hadn't met any of the kids around town yet, but she knew there had to be someone she'd feel a connection with. After all, this was a farming community; and farms meant animals, and animals meant others who shared her love of them.

Melody's mother got up to leave. "One other thing," she said, "where would you keep a horse if you had one? The town authorities would frown if we tried to keep a horse on this small lot."

"Abby boards horses. And I've seen places near town where a horse could be kept."

"Just remember, the cost of a horse doesn't stop with buying it. There will be board, feed, vet bills, shoeing, and all those kinds of things."

"I know."

The first day of school dawned clear and bright. After long deliberation, Melody decided on a simple shirt and a new pair of stone-washed jeans. She fixed a new clip to hold her medium long hair behind her neck. Looking into the mirror, she wondered if she should have some lipstick to put on. Did girls in seventh grade wear makeup in this town? At her other schools, it hadn't been allowed; but she had heard it said you didn't fit in at public schools if you didn't wear some kind of makeup. Oh, well, it was too late to do anything about it now; besides, she didn't even have a lipstick to her name, and she didn't like the colors of the one or two she saw her mother wear occasionally.

"You look nice," Mrs. Morrison said when Melody entered the tiny kitchen.

"Thanks, Mom." The girl took a plate and spooned a helping of scrambled eggs on it and grabbed a few slices of bacon. "Mom, do you think I should wear some makeup?"

"You don't need makeup," her dad said from behind his paper.

"Now, Craig, we don't know what the customs at this school are." Mrs. Morrison turned to Melody. "Look around today and notice what the others are wearing," she said, "and if you need a lipstick or light foundation, we'll see about getting some after school."

"Jen, you're spoiling that girl!"

"It's hard enough starting a new school without being out of step with the regular students. Remember, she's going to a public school now, not a tightly regulated private school."

"Makes no difference. Girls her age don't need to be painting their faces."

"Dad!"

Mr. Morrison laid his paper down and glared at Melody. "Young lady, you may be going to a public school now, but that is no reason for you to put aside the values you've learned up until now."

"Craig, she's only talking about a little lipstick and maybe some light powder or liquid foundation. What harm can that do?" Mrs. Morrison asked.

"I will hear no more about this," Mr. Morrison said. He picked up the paper and resumed reading.

Melody pushed her half-eaten breakfast away from her. "I've gotta go," she mumbled. "Bye, Mom. Bye, Dad."

Melody was out the door before her father could say more. She knew her mom would continue to stick up for her, but in the end they would most likely both bow to his wishes. It wasn't that her dad was mean; he was just so out of touch with what young people faced these days. Too many times Melody listened to him tell how it was when he went to school, and expound on why he saw no reason for it to be any different for her brothers or for her. She sympathized with why both Randy and Jeff had been so eager to leave home once they were out of school.

"Hi. You're new aren't you?"

Turning, Melody saw a heavy-set girl with short dark hair approaching her. The girl's moon face was open and friendly, and she was flashing one of the prettiest smiles Melody had ever seen.

"I'm Carol Anderson," the girl said. "I live over on the next block. I saw when you and your folks moved in."

"I'm Melody. Melody Morrison."

Carol slowed to keep pace with Melody. For as large as she was, she walked surprisingly fast. "Where did you move from?"

"Seattle. But before that we lived in Montana."

"Why did you ever move to Seattle?" Carol asked.

"My dad wanted to finish his degree so he could teach at a university," Melody said. "So we sold everything we had when I was six and moved. I hated it. We had to leave all the dogs and cats behind and my pet goat, Bouncer."

"I think I would have hated it, too," Carol said, and again she smiled. Melody liked her.

The school was only three blocks from the Morrison's house. Melody and Carol approached the old, one-story cement block building along with several other students who walked from home. Orange-yellow school buses were disgorging their passengers midst shouts of greeting and chatting about what each had done over the summer. A nearby parking lot was rapidly filling with assorted vehicles, most of which were pickup trucks ranging from very old and battered to bright and shining new. A blue truck with gleaming silver trim narrowly missed the girls as it swerved into the lot, showering them with gravel.

"That's the Farrady boys," Carol said. "Their family owns a lot of land around here, and they think they can lord it over everyone else. Their dad gave Ralph that truck when he turned sixteen. His brother, Rupert, will be in our class, unfortunately."

Melody didn't have time to ask why Carol thought that way about Rupert. The first bell rang and everyone scrambled to get to their rooms on time.

"Hey, you can't have that seat," a gruff voice behind Melody said as she was about to slide in a place behind Carol.

She turned and looked into the gray eyes of a boy several inches taller than she was. He would have been good looking if it wasn't for the scowl that seemed to be imprinted permanently on his face.

"Why not?"

"Because this is MY seat," he said, shoving Melody aside and sitting in her place.

Hot tears stung Melody's eyes as she moved to take a seat the next row over. She wasn't used to this kind of behavior from classmates. She had always been taught the importance of good manners and consideration for others. She fought to keep the hurt from overflowing. It would never do to let her new classmates see her cry.

"That wasn't your seat, Rupert," Carol said.

So that's Rupert, Melody thought.

"Well, it's my seat now, isn't it, Tubbalina?"

Snickers echoed around the room. Melody's temper flared. "You have no right to call her names!"

"Let it be, Melody," Carol said quietly. "It doesn't matter."

Melody looked at Carol's red face and too-bright eyes. "It does matter. They have no right to make fun of you or any one else."

"What are you, a preacher's kid?" Rupert sneered. "Is that why your name is Melody? You're going to sing us a song about what's not allowed?"

"I'm not a preacher's kid," Melody said, "but I do know what's right and what's wrong. And it's wrong to make fun of people."

"Oooooooooooo . . . . . ." she heard from around room.

"Melody's going to sing us a song," a blonde-haired girl in the back chanted. "She's going to tell us when we do something wrong."

"Oooooooooooo . . . .."

"Enough!" The voice was quiet, yet it oozed with authority.

Melody turned as a man built like a Sumo wrestler entered the room. She figured he must be the math teacher.

"In your seats and quiet it down," he commanded. He didn't raise his voice; he didn't need to. "Rupert, you sit down in this front row."

Rupert's scowl deepened, but he did as he was told; but not before he made an obscene gesture toward Melody that only the class could see. He didn't get the reaction he wanted from her, as she didn't understand what he did.

Melody slid into the seat he vacated and squeezed the hand Carol offered to her.

Melody could hardly wait for school to let out. Rupert was in two of her classes, both of which fortunately had strong teachers who didn't let him get away with much when they were around. But the halls between classes were another matter. If it had been only him and what he said to her, it might have been bearable; but several of the boys and some girls followed his lead and taunted both Melody and Carol throughout the day. The refrains of "Melody's going to sing us a song. She's going to tell us when we do something wrong," followed her wherever she walked. She learned the girl who started it was Jean Monroe, another one whose family was big in the valley and who felt she could act any way she pleased.

However, the very worse for Melody to endure was the amount of foul language she heard the kids speaking to each other. It seemed every other word began with "f" or "s." Such words were never spoken in the Morrison house, and would never be tolerated in the private schools she had attended. She wondered what kind of homes some of her classmates came from.

That night when Mrs. Morrison asked how school went, Melody said very little. She did tell about Carol and how she liked her, but she never said anything about the name calling and bad language. She wanted to handle the problem with Rupert and Jean by herself. And she didn't want her parents to know the kinds of words she was being exposed to.

CHAPTER FOUR:
OPPORTUNITY

Melody hated school. Oh, her classes were all right, and she liked all her teachers, especially Mrs. Watkins in art and Mr. Samson in math. Carol turned out to be a wonderful friend. It was most of the other kids that made it so miserable for her. Rupert and Jean never lost an opportunity to sing-song their little rhyme whenever Melody was within hearing distance. Soon others were following suit. The foul language continued to rankle her. On occasion she found herself almost using one or more of the words.

"How can you stand them calling you names all the time?" she asked Carol one day as they walked home together. "And the words they use when they talk! It's like they only know about five or six words, all of them I wouldn't dare say in front of my folks.

"It only makes matters worse if I say anything," Carol said. "I try to ignore them as much as possible. I know what you mean about the language. I've slipped up at home a couple of times."

"What do you do when you can't stand it anymore?"

"Go have a good cry," Carol answered quietly. "Then I imagine how ugly Rupert is going to look by the time he's thirty because his face is going to be set in that ugly expression of his. Then I imagine Jean being bald because she has to have chemotherapy or some such thing as that. You know how stuck up she is about her hair."

"That's awful!" Melody giggled. "It would serve them right, though, if those things happened." She fell silent for a moment. "I shouldn't have said that; it wasn't very nice."

"Maybe not," Carol agreed. "But nasty people don't deserve nice thoughts."

"Still, it wasn't right of me to say it."

The weekends were Melody's sanity salvation. That was when she and Mom would go out to Abby's. She felt sorry that her mother had to be cooped up in the house working on Abby's books and correspondence while she was outside enjoying the horses and dogs. But it wasn't all play for Melody either. She had stalls and pens to clean, saddles and bridles to shampoo and condition, and horses to groom.

All the time she would be doing those things, Mick would shadow her every move. Every so often he would place a paw against her leg or a cold nose in her hand to catch her attention and get a hug and petting. While Melody had her riding lesson on Miss Piggy, he would lie outside the round pen or arena, depending which area was being used.

Melody's absolute favorite time, however, was when she could spend time with Dancer. The young horse would follow her every footstep when she was cleaning the stall and pen, and would make the funniest faces when Melody scratched certain spots. Melody laughed when Dancer positioned herself to catch the pulsating stream from the irrigation sprinkler on hot days. The other horses would steer clear of the shooting water, but Dancer deliberately sought it out, twisting and turning to get wet all over.

Whenever Abby worked with Dancer, Melody stopped whatever she was doing and watched. One day Abby buckled something that looked like a belt around the horse just behind the front legs. She attached two long lines to each side of the halter and passed the ends through rings that were fastened to each side of the belt-like thing and brought them to the back of the horse.

"What's that?" Melody asked.

"That's a surcingle," Abby said, "and these are driving reins."

"What are you going to do?"

"This is called ground driving," Abby said. She stepped behind Dancer, picked up the lines and made a clucking sound. Dancer moved forward with Abby walking behind her. By pulling on first one line then the other, Abby was able to command Dancer to go different directions. She pulled both lines and kissed, and Dancer backed up. "This starts a horse learning to obey the commands given through reins," Abby explained. "It's useful whether you're training for the saddle or for harness."

"Can I try it?" Melody asked.

"Sure. Here."

Melody took the long reins and clucked to Dancer. The horse sensed someone different behind her. She turned her head and fixed one large eye on the girl. She nickered softly, then faced front and began walking. Dancer responded to the lightest pressure on the reins. She and Melody walked figure eights and around various obstacles in the barnyard. Watching from one side, Abby nodded several times in approval when Melody guided the filly in particularly difficult maneuvers..

"She responds well to you. You've got a good hand."

Melody blushed. "She knows I like her. I think she'd do anything I asked of her."

"You may be right. There does seem to be a connection between you." Abby began removing the long reins and surcingle.

"Abby, I know you said a green rider and a green horse shouldn't be put together, but aren't there exceptions?"

"Sometimes people get away with it. But most of the time it's a disaster."

"But if they both were trained by an experienced person, wouldn't it work?"

Abby neatly wound the reins and clipped them to one of the rings on the surcingle. "I suppose."

By this time Melody had snapped the cross ties to Dancer's halter and began brushing the red-gold coat.

"You really like that filly, don't you?" Abby said after watching Melody groom the horse a few minutes.

"Oh, yes! I dream about her all the time."

"Most girls your age are infatuated with horses. It will pass."

"No, it won't!" Melody protested. She laid her face against the warm flank and felt the movement of the horse's easy breathing.

"Isn't there some way I could buy her? I could get a job and save my money."

"Twenty-four hundred is a lot for someone your age to save up."

"I could do it," Melody said. "I know I can."

"Let's wait and see," Abby said, opening Dancer's stall door for her. "We'll see what happens in a few months. Then we'll talk again."

"Does that mean you'll let me buy her?"

"I said we'll talk again in a few months."

Why is it grownups think we kids can't do anything? Melody wondered. She took a manure fork down from its nail on a post and set to work lifting out the wet spots and manure from the sawdust bedding in the stalls. She stopped to look at Dancer, whose eyes followed her every move down the row. "We'll show them, girl," she said. "They'll see. Someday you'll be mine."

Actually, Abby hadn't said no when I asked about buying Dancer, Melody reflected. *I take that as a good sign. Next I have to find a job so I can start saving up. Now, what can a thirteen-year-old do?*

"Mom, can you give me some ideas what kind of work I could do to earn money?" Melody asked as they drove back to town.

"Still thinking about buying a horse?"

"Not just any horse. Dancer. Oh, Mom, she's the most beautiful horse I've ever seen. And she likes me. I know she does."

"Love at first klonk, huh?"

Melody rubbed the top of her head as she remembered her first meeting with Dancer. "I guess. Anyway, I know she's the horse for me."

"What does Abby say?"

"She said we'd talk about it in a few months. She thinks it's just a passing fad."

"She may be right."

"It's not a fad! I know it's not."

"We'll see."

"Mom! That's not fair! You know I love horses. I've always loved them."   •

Mrs. Morrison smiled. "I know. You and I are just alike in that respect."

"Then you know how I feel."

"Yes. Yes, I do." Melody's mother fell silent a couple of moments. "Okay, I'll help you try to find a job. There has to be something kids your age can do. You'll know soon enough if your love for horses is the real thing, or, as Abby says, a passing fad."

Melody threw her arm across her mother's shoulders and hugged her. "Thanks, Mom." She grew silent; then asked, "What about Dad? What will he say?"

"We'll cross that bridge when we come to it. First you have to find a job and begin saving your money. And don't forget about prayer."

"I've been praying every night," Melody said.

A couple of evenings later while at the dinner table, Mr. Morrison surprised all of them by saying, "Melody, I understand you want to earn some money."

"I've been thinking about it."

"Well, how would you like to do a paper route here in town?"

"I didn't know one was available," Melody said.

"It wasn't until today. The carrier was collecting and I asked him how old one had to be to do a route."

"What did he say?"

"He said he was twelve when the paper hired him."

"Is there a route available?" Melody could hardly contain her excitement.

"As a matter of fact, there is," her father said with infuriating slowness.

"When?"

"His dad has been transferred and he needs a replacement by the end of next week."

Her heart racing with excitement, Melody asked, "How do I go about getting it?"

Mr. Morrison reached in his shirt pocket and pulled out a

neatly folded piece of paper. He slowly unfolded it and handed it
to Melody. "There's his name and phone number."

Without taking time to excuse herself from the table, Melody
ran to the phone and dialed the number. A few minutes later, her
face aglow, she returned to the table.

"Well?" her mother asked.

"I go out with him after school tomorrow," Melody said.

"How much time will it take you?"

"Brian said it takes about two hours after school during the
week, and about three hours early Sunday morning starting about
five o'clock."

"Will you be able to do that?"

"All I have to do is set my alarm," Melody said. "And I'll be
done in plenty of time for Sunday School. Also, I won't have papers to deliver on Saturday, so we'll still be able to go out to Abby's."

"It's a big commitment you'll be taking on," Mr. Morrison
said. "It's going to have to be your responsibility. There won't be
any shoving it off on your mom or me to do it for you like Randy
tried to do with his route."

"Dad, I'm not like that!" *Gee, he can be so exasperating*, Melody
thought. *Just because my brother got tired of his route and had to be
prodded into doing it doesn't mean I'm was going to be the same way.*

Later when Melody was helping her mother clean the kitchen,
she said, "Mom, I think the first part of my prayer has been answered."

Mrs. Morrison smiled. "You may be right."

That night Melody's dreams were filled with her sitting astride
Dancer, racing over the sage-covered hills that surrounded the valley.
She could feel the wind whipping the auburn-colored mane back into
her face as she and the red dun horse moved together as one.

CHAPTER FIVE:
THE DEBT

"Careful. That dog bites," Brian warned.

Melody hesitated, her hand on the gate. A dog kooking like a cross between a husky and something else sat on the steps and watched her. He wasn't growling, and he gazed at her steadily. Melody could detect no fear in his eyes nor aggression in his posture. She decided to take a chance and opened the gate. Walking forward a few steps, she crouched and held her hand out, palm up, fingers slightly curled.

The dog eyed Melody a moment longer, then slowly he left the steps and approached her. He sniffed her hand, then licked her fingers.

Laughing softly, Melody reached behind the dog's ear and rubbed. His tail began wagging, and the licking became broad, wet strokes.

"Well, I'll be . . ." she heard someone say. "Who might you be?"

Melody looked up and saw a man with a black moustache, clad in torn jeans and a dirty T-shirt, standing in the doorway. "I'm Melody Morrison," she said in a small voice, standing. "I'm going to be doing this paper route." She approached the house and timidly held the paper out to him. His dog followed at her heels, his tail continuing to wag.

The man took the paper. "What'd you feed my dog?" he growled.

"Nothing."

"You had to feed him something. He don't cotton to no strangers."

"Honest, mister, she didn't feed him anything." Brian said from outside the fence. "She just opened the gate and walked in."

The man appraised the girl before him. Her hazel eyes looked straight back into his. A half smile began softening his harsh features. "Rogue's pretty choosy who he trusts. Guess you're okay." He turned and strode back into the house.

"How did you do that?" Brian asked once Melody was back by his side.

"Do what?"

"Get that dog to like you. He always growls at me. I never go inside the gate. I just toss the paper on the porch and hope I don't miss."

Melody shrugged. "Animals just seem to like me."

Delivering the papers took considerably longer than the two hours Brian promised it would take, but Melody knew once she memorized where all the customers lived, she'd be able to do it in a much shorter time. Already she was planning how to more efficiently walk the route so there would be less backtracking. She was glad neither Rupert nor Jean lived in town. At least she wouldn't have to chance facing them after school.

Melody met some of the customers while Brian showed her around. Most of them were quite elderly, having chosen to live out their retirement years in this small central Washington town, or else they were unable to afford moving to a warmer climate. Because of their limited mobility, their papers were placed between the storm and regular doors or in boxes on porches. This made more work for the carrier; but unlike Brian who chaffed at doing anything extra, Melody didn't mind. She had a special spot in her heart for elderly people, especially since she seldom saw either of her grandmothers and both grandfathers had died before her parents even met.

The most memorable customer Melody met that day was Mrs. Nenana. The woman was barely five feet tall. She wore her silvery hair in a twisted bun at the back of her head, and she had on a long skirt and blouse with Native American designs woven into it. Long silver and turquoise earrings dangled from her ears.

"I hope you'll be getting my paper to me at a reasonable time," Mrs. Nenana said when Brian introduced Melody to her. Brian's face reddened.

"Yes, ma'am," Melody said.

"And be sure you put it between the doors and close the outer door tight. I don't want the wind banging it around."

"Yes, ma'am."

"And don't go slamming the door. Sometimes I'm asleep and it may be the only sleep I've had all day."

"No, ma'am," Melody said. "I'll be quiet."

Mrs. Nenana looked at her sharply. "You're new in town, aren't you?"

"Yes, ma'am."

"Where did you move from?"

"Seattle. But before that we lived in Montana, near Bozeman."

"Well, you seem to be a polite little thing. Maybe you'll do." Mrs. Nenana took the paper and went back inside her house.

The hardest part of delivering papers was getting up at five o'clock on Sunday mornings, especially with the sun rising later each day. But the photograph of Dancer that Melody kept by her clock radio spurred her past the temptation to linger a few minutes longer under the warm covers.

The Sunday paper was considerably heavier than the weekday issues, and Mrs. Morrison took it upon herself to drive Melody around on the route. Her father protested, saying Melody was going to be spoiled; but his words were ignored. Melody was grateful to her mom; for without her help, the Sunday edition would never be delivered in time for her to get ready for church.

School continued to be a miserable existence for Melody. Carol, who was also an outcast, was her only friend. All the others either followed Rupert's and Jean's lead and made fun of her every chance they could, or else they avoided her so the stigma wouldn't rub off on them. Melody bottled her feelings up inside, except for sharing them with Carol. She didn't want her parents worrying about her.

Melody lived for Saturday. That was the one day of the week

she had neither school nor papers to deliver. Her mother would drive her out to Abby's ranch early in the morning. Sometimes she stayed to do work for Abby, but often she left Melody there until late afternoon. More than the riding lesson each time, Melody looked forward to the time she could spend with Dancer. No horse on Abby's ranch had a more carefully cleaned stall, and no horse was groomed as lovingly as was Dancer. And no horse received as many carrots or apples as Dancer did. Yet, for all the time she spent with the horse, Melody was careful to do all the chores Abby lined up for her, as well as anything else she saw that needed doing and that was within her capabilities.

One Saturday toward mid-October, Melody noticed one of the dogs was missing.

"Abby, where's Mick?"

"I sold him to a sheep herder," Abby answered.

"You sold him?" There was an accusatory tone in Melody's voice.

"He wasn't a pet, Mel. He was bred and raised to be a working stock dog."

"But, why him? He didn't act like the other dogs. He only wanted to love and be loved."

"Because he's the only one that wasn't one of my breeding dogs," Abby said. "Besides, he's quiet around sheep." She walked away to do something else.

Melody missed Mick. Although all the dogs greeted her enthusiastically each time she arrived at the ranch, Mick had been the one who stayed close by her in everything she did. The rest of the dogs went off with Abby to move cattle or to follow her when she worked on the irrigation or did other things in the fields.

"Well, at least I still have you," Melody said to Dancer, laying her cheek against the horse's velvety muzzle. Dancer "whuffed", tickling her ear.

The following day Mrs. Morrison received a phone call just as the family finished Sunday dinner. Melody overheard her say, "We'll be there in about an hour."

"Who was that?" Melody asked when her mother returned the receiver to its cradle.

"Abby. She wants us to come out so she can talk with the two of us."

"Did she say why?"

"Something about a debt and a horse. But that was all she said."

"She didn't say it was about Dancer, did she?"

"No. Now let's get these dishes done so we can go."

What did Abby want to talk to them about? Melody wondered as she helped clear away the dishes. *Is she going to talk about me being able to buy Dancer? Maybe that was it! Maybe Abby saw how serious I am about working in order to buy the horse that now she is going to let me buy Dancer on payments. Yes, that has to be it.*

The ride to the ranch seemed to take longer than usual. Melody reflected on the first time she had ridden this way with her mother. Little had she realized she was going to meet the horse of her dreams. Now, they were going to talk with Abby about her buying the horse. Melody figured how much she had saved from the paper route already and how much she could save each month. If Abby hadn't upped the price on the horse, by this time next year Dancer could be all hers.

The smell of warm apple sauce and cinnamon greeted Melody and her mother when they entered Abby's spacious kitchen. Row upon row of gleaming jars filled with golden brown applesauce sat upon one long counter. A partially empty basket of apples sat in the middle of the floor, and a heap of apple peelings filled a colander in the sink. Melody knew the horses would be getting a treat with their hay and grain that evening.

Abby motioned for them to sit at the white-enameled table where a steaming teapot and cups had been placed. She placed a plate of warm apple cake before them and sat down.

"Mel," Abby began in a quieter than normal voice, "I know you've had your heart set on being able to buy Dancer."

Melody's eyes lit up. *Here it comes*, she thought. *She's going to tell me I can.*

"And I know," Abby continued, "that I've told you green horses and green riders don't mix very well, . . ."

But we do, Melody thought. *We get along like we were made for each other.* She could hardly contain her excitement.

" . . .but that's not the reason I won't be able to sell her to you," Abby finished.

The fork in Melody's hand dropped with a clatter to the plate, the piece of apple cake bounced off and fell to the floor where one of the dogs snatched it up. "But, why?"

Abby turned slightly and stared out the window which over-looked the sweep of land toward the forested hills. Her eyes shone brightly and her upper lip trembled slightly. "You know my husband died suddenly a couple of years ago," she said. "He didn't have his affairs in very good order. That's why I've had your mother going over the books and other papers for me. We thought we discovered all the debts and had taken care of them, but . . ." Abby's voice broke slightly. She punched tears out of her eyes and continued, " . . .another creditor came to light last night."

Mrs. Morrison rose and stood behind Abby. She placed a comforting hand on her shoulder.

"My husband borrowed money from this man to pay for the hay we needed two years ago. When I told him I had no money with which to pay him right now, he demanded that I give him Dancer in payment, or else he'd take me to court."

Hot tears filled Melody's eyes. "Will he take payments?" she asked. "I have over two hundred dollars already saved up. And I can pay that much each month."

"I already told him someone wanted the horse and that it would be a while before I had the money. But he said the loan is long overdue and he wants payment now." Abby turned toward Melody. "I'm sorry, Mel. I really am. I was wanting to see you earn Dancer. I think you and she would have been the exception."

Melody got up from the table and walked into the living room. She stood at the large picture window and looked out at the pasture where Dancer and Miss Piggy were contentedly grazing. Tears she no longer tried to hold back streamed down her cheeks. She watched her dream lift her head and look toward the house. *Oh, Dancer!* she cried inwardly. *I want you so much!* She felt her mother's arm around her shoulder and allowed herself to be pulled into an embrace.

"Oh, Mom! Is it really true? Does Abby really have to give Dancer to that man?"

"I'm afraid so.'

"Couldn't we get a loan or something so Abby can pay him, and I'll pay it off?" She looked up into her mother's face, which had become as equally wet as her own.

"I already called and asked your dad," Mrs. Morrison said. "You know what his answer was."

Melody turned back to the window. Dancer was floating across the pasture with that incredibly smooth jog of hers. *Gads, she is beautiful!*

"There are other horses, you know," her mother said. "You could save your money and buy a more broke horse for maybe a lot less. Abby says there's a big horse sale every spring down in Oregon where you might find a horse just right for you."

"But it wouldn't be Dancer. It just wouldn't be the same." Melody looked out the window another minute. "Can we go now, Mom?"

Mrs. Morrison looked over at Abby who was standing in the living room doorway. Abby nodded. "Okay," her mother said. "We can go."

Her face wet and her nose dripping uncontrollably, Melody stared out the car window. "Mom?"

"Yes?"

"If God wanted me to have that paper route after I asked Him for a job so I could buy Dancer, then why did He take Dancer away from me?"

"I don't know. We can't know why God does everything He does. All I do know is He has His reasons." Mrs. Morrison took her eyes off the road briefly and reached over to lay a hand on Melody's leg. "Sometimes all we can do is trust that He knows what's best for us."

That night Melody didn't sleep. Over and over she replayed the events of the afternoon. She had been so sure Abby was wanting to talk with them about her buying Dancer. Who was this man the debt was owed to? Why did he have to show up now when she finally had a way to earn money to buy the red dun filly? And why wouldn't her dad help? At times it seemed as if he didn't care about what mattered to her or her mother. And why did God let her think He had answered her prayer about being able to buy Dancer and then take the horse away? Life just wasn't fair.

CHAPTER SIX:
"WHACK!"

Melody's eyes were red-rimmed and swollen the following morning. The last thing she wanted was to face Rupert and Jean. They would take one look at her face and know something was wrong, and they would be sure to try to make her feel even worse than she already did.

A cold, wet washcloth helped somewhat to lessen the redness, but hours would be needed to reduce the puffiness. Maybe she could say she was having an allergic reaction. It wouldn't be the truth, but getting teased about that would be better than being mocked for crying. As long as she didn't think about Dancer—tears filled her eyes again—she'd make it through the day.

"Aren't you going to eat breakfast?" Mrs. Morrison asked when Melody walked toward the door carrying her book bag.

"I'm not hungry right now. I'll get something to eat during break."

Melody's mother looked at her daughter's face. "I understand," she said quietly. "Go before your dad comes down."

"Thanks, Mom."

The sky was sullen gray and a mist hung in the air. *Just how I feel*, Melody thought. Her feet dragged as she walked the short distance from her house to the corner where Carol was waiting.

Carol looked closely at Melody. "Want to talk about it?" she asked.

"I can't just yet," Melody said. "Maybe later." She fought to keep from crying again.

"Okay. Just let me know when."

That was the nice thing about Carol, Melody thought. *She's there when you need someone to talk with, but she doesn't pry if you want to be left alone. And she never, ever gossips or breaks confidences.*

"What are you going to say to Jean or Rupert if they start in?"

"You mean 'when they start in,' don't you?" Melody said. "I'll just say I'm having an allergic reaction." *Which I guess isn't really a lie,* she finished to herself. *I am having a reaction to not being able to buy Dancer.* Tears brightened her eyes. She bowed her head, but not before Carol saw.

"Do you want a latte before class? My treat."

Melody loved the flavored espresso coffee and steamed milk drink she had been introduced to in Seattle. When she discovered the Future Farmers of America Club operated an espresso stand in the mornings as a fund raiser, she was one of their most frequent customers until she began saving every penny toward buying Dancer.

"Not today. Thanks."

"Okay. Let me know if you change your mind."

They walked the rest of the way in silence. Melody desperately wanted to skip school; but if she did that, she'd be found out for sure and her dad would blow a gasket. Both her brothers had skipped classes a lot and had almost blown their chances to graduate. Melody wanted to go to college, and she knew skipping classes would jeopardize her chances.

"What? No song from Melody today?" Rupert leaned against the locker next to Melody's. He took in her red, puffy eyes. "What happened?" he sneered. "Daddy catch his little girl being bad?"

"Leave it alone, Rupert!" Carol snapped.

"Why should I? I don't listen to a Tubbalina."

Melody turned and faced Rupert squarely. In a very low, tightly controlled voice, she said, "One of these days, someone is going to put you in your place, Rupert Farrady."

"Ooooo, I'm scared. I'm so scared." Rupert pretended to reel back under Melody's words. Snickers broke out along the hallway.

The situation may have become worse, except the bell rang for first class. Students scattered to their respective rooms. Melody and Carol fast walked to the art room. Art was Melody's favorite class, in spite of Jean Monroe being in it, too. Mrs. Watkins didn't tolerate negative talk or behavior toward others. What Melody liked best, however, was that Mrs. Watkins knew how to challenge the students to try things they never thought possible. Melody had discovered a talent for art she didn't know she possessed. Today, though, she really didn't want to be in this class. The picture she was working on was a composite of Dancer in various activities.

Melody stood before the rack of unfinished paintings. She knew exactly which one was hers, but she didn't reach for it. She jumped when Mrs. Watkins spoke behind her.

"Melody, would you like to help me with a project?"

"Sure." Grateful for the reprise, Melody followed the teacher into the store room. From floor to ceiling in the narrow room, shelves were crammed with boxes, some several years old, and piles of papers all different sizes and color, and jars and tubes of paint, and other unidentifiable items.

Mrs. Watkins waved her arm to indicate the area. "The school board has asked for an inventory of what I have in supplies and a list of what I think we'll need." She looked at Melody. If she noticed the red eyes, she made no mention of it. "You're further ahead on your project than the others. I was wondering if you'd be willing to work on taking an inventory for me?"

Melody almost sighed with relief. "I'll be glad to." Good. This job would take a few days at least, a few days she could avoid working on her painting. She took the clipboard from Mrs. Watkins. Several sheets of a computer-generated form were attached to it. Mrs. Watkins told her how she wanted the information recorded, then she left Melody alone.

The noise of students working in the adjoining room became no more than a low din. Melody found herself enjoying exploration of the store room. A surprising number of different art supplies were stored on the shelves. She found some that were so old they were no longer useful. These she placed in a box by the door.

"How is it going?" Mrs. Watkins asked when the period was nearly up.

"Okay." Melody pointed to the box of discards. "Those are no good for one reason or another."

"I forgot to tell you I wanted you to do just that. Thanks."
Mrs. Watkins smiled. "How much longer do you think it will
take?"

Melody looked around the room. "About three or four more
days, I think."

"Would you mind finishing it? I could get someone else to
help, but you know exactly which areas you've done. Besides, you
know what you're looking at. Some people can't tell one brush
from another, let alone one medium from another."

"I'll be glad to," Melody said. She wondered if Mrs. Watkins
knew something about what had happened with Dancer or if this
were just a coincidence. Mom was always saying there were no
such things as coincidences, only God's incidences. It didn't really
matter. What mattered was she wouldn't have to face that painting
this week at least.

One class down, six to go, Melody thought, walking to her
locker to get her English book. She worked the combination to the
lock and opened the door. Dancer's picture hung on the inside at
eye level.

"I hear your horse is going to go to pay off a debt," she heard
Rupert say.

Swiveling around, Melody looked into his leering features.
"Who told you that?" she demanded.

"Oh, word gets around. My uncle Roland's the one who's taking her."

Melody's heart pounded. *A Farrady taking my beloved Dancer!
That can't be!* She fought the tears, but it was no use; they came
anyway.

"Look at the cry baby!" Rupert said loudly. "Crying over a
stupid horse."

She didn't remember grabbing the book. Melody gripped the
English text with both hands, her knuckles white. Without another thought to what she was doing nor of the possible conse-
quences, she whirled around, raised her hands and, with all the

force she could muster, brought the book crashing down on Rupert's head. "Whack!" The two-inch thick book bent in the middle.

Rupert staggered back. For a moment Melody thought he would go down. He leaned against the bank of lockers, holding the top of his head with both hands. Gasps and murmurings sounded up and down the hall. Shaking, Melody walked up to Rupert and placed her face inches from his. "I've had all I'm going to take from you, Rupert Farrady," she said in a low voice. "You think you can get away with making fun of people just because your family owns half the valley. You are nothing but a bully, and no one likes bullies."

Melody grabbed her books and ran for the girls' restroom. The second bell for class rang, but she didn't pay attention to it. Sobs shook her whole body as she gave in to her pent up emotions. *Why did he have to tease me about Dancer? I just can't take any more of his nastiness,* she told herself. *I've tried to ignore him, but today was just too much. Poor Dancer! I don't want to see her going to a Farrady. And Rupert knows it. I've tried to ignore him and stay out of his way, but he keeps seeking me out. Now I've lost my temper and hit him. I'm going to be in big trouble. What will Mom and Dad say? What will Dad do?*

A hand touched her shoulder. She looked up to see Carol, and another girl standing there. Both of them were grinning.

"What's so funny?" Melody demanded.

"I think Rupert is going to have one granddaddy of a head-ache," the other girl said. She reached over and picked up Melody's English book and showed it to her. "Look what you did."

Melody looked at the book. The spine was noticeably bent, and a line showed where the underlying cardboard had broken beneath the cloth on the front cover. "I did that?"

Carol nodded.

"I'm really in trouble now," Melody said.

"But he deserved it," Carol said. "If you hadn't done it, some-one else would have sooner or later."

"That's not the point. I'm the one who hit him, not someone else." Melody wet a paper towel and wiped her face, hoping the cold water would erase the signs of her crying. She picked up her books and started to leave.

"Where are you going?" the other girl asked. Melody thought her name was Denise, or something like that.

"To the office."

"Why?"

"To tell what happened. It's better to confess to something you've done wrong before you're accused of it."

"I wouldn't," Carol said. "There were no teachers around, and I don't think Rupert's going to tattle. If he did, it would come out just how mean he's been to you and practically everyone else not in his little group."

"No, I've got to do what I think is right."

Mrs. Watkins was in the school office talking with Mr. Wentworth when Melody entered the room. Melody swallowed hard. "I've got to report something I did," she said.

The teacher and principal looked at each other, then at Melody.

"Come into the office," Mr. Wentworth said. "You, too, Mrs. Watkins." He closed the door and motioned for them to sit. "Okay, tell me what's happened."

Melody held out her English book. "I hit Rupert over the head."

A stifled laugh came from Mrs. Watkins. She quickly covered her mouth with a hand to hide the smile that played on her lips. Mr. Wentworth took the book and looked at it closely, turning it over and fingering the bent spine and cracked cover.

"I know I'll have to pay for the book," Melody said. "It was wrong for me to hit him."

"Why did you hit him?" Mr. Wentworth asked. His voice was kind, not angry at all. He handed the book to Mrs. Watkins.

"He was calling me names and taunting me. He's called me names from the very first day of school, and today I just couldn't take it any more."

"Mrs. Watkins, do you know anything about this?"

Laughter glinted in the teacher's eyes, but the rest of her

expression was under control. "Rupert Farrady has been a bully since kindergarten," she said. "No one has dared to stand up to him because his family provides so many jobs around here. I would say he got what he's been asking for." She turned to Melody. "Was he still standing after you hit him?"

"Yes. But I think his head hurts."

"I bet it is!" She turned back to Mr. Wentworth. "You're new here, so you don't know all the politics involving some of the big families in this area. I suggest we just let the matter rest unless Rupert decides to press the issue. Somehow, I don't think he will."

"What about the book?" Melody asked.

"It was damaged when you got it," Mrs. Watkins said matter-of-factly, handing it back to her. "Don't worry about it. Now, get to your class."

All eyes were upon Melody as she entered the room. One or two of the kids actually had friendly smiles for her. Rupert, however, didn't look in her direction.

Melody stopped by his desk. In a voice only he could hear, she said, "I'm sorry. I shouldn't have hit you so hard."

Rupert looked up, his eyes wide with a combination of pain and surprise. He searched her face. She looked steadily back at him. "Guess I asked for it," he grunted.

"You did," Melody said. She took her seat next to Carol.

CHAPTER SEVEN: MICK

Melody continued having difficulty holding back tears whenever she thought about Dancer. However, she did have a certain satisfaction in how things turned out between her and Rupert. Other than admitting he probably asked for the English book over his head, he made no other mention of the incident to either Melody or to his friends. But, he no longer called either Melody or Carol names. When his friends started to, he would tell them to back off. School became bearable for Melody.

At first Melody wanted to quit the paper route. She knew she had to give a month's notice, and was about to do so, when her mother suggested she keep it until the end of the year, at least. That way she'd have spending money for Christmas. Melody agreed, but reluctantly.

Abby also convinced Melody to continue with her riding lessons. "After all," she said, "the way you love horses, you'll be getting one sooner or later." Therefore, Melody and her mother kept going out to the ranch on Saturdays.

An unusually wet weather system spread over the Northwest, bringing days of rain to this normally dry area east of the Cascades Mountains. The road leading to Abby's ranch became slick with the clay-like mud which formed. Mrs. Morrison was able to negotiate the little Geo along it only by staying out of the deep ruts. Occasionally the little car would slip into a hole and get stuck, then Melody would have to get out and push. Some days she arrived at the ranch muddier than when she left it.

Until the road dried or froze over, Rupert's uncle wasn't able to bring his horse trailer in to take possession of Dancer. Once her chores were done and after she had her riding lesson, Melody spent every spare moment she could with the young horse.

Sometimes Abby let Melody do the training exercises with Dancer. She watched the girl and horse work together, a thoughtful look coming over her face. Abby wasn't one to do a great deal of talking, but she became even more quiet during this time.

Especially heavy rain continued to fall during November. One Saturday it came down in sheets, and Abby called to tell Mrs. Morrison to not try driving all the way to the ranch. She would meet them at the cattle guard with her four-wheel drive vehicle.

"At least I know that man hasn't taken Dancer yet," Melody said as she and her mother waited in the foggy windowed car a little later. "I hope he can never get in to take her."

"That's a little unreasonable, isn't it?" her mother asked. "Sooner or later this rain will either stop, or the weather will get cold enough to freeze the mud."

"I keep hoping and praying something will happen that will let me get her after all." Melody wiped a clearing in the window and looked out. "Mom, look! What's that over there?"

Mrs. Morrison looked where her daughter was pointing. A black and white heap lay by the edge of the ditch a short distance beyond the cattle guard. "I think it's a dog. He's not moving. Wait, Melody!"

But the girl was already out of the car and running toward the still form. *Oh, God*, she cried inwardly, *don't let it be dead!* Kneeling beside the still body, she saw that it was a dog. Somehow it looked familiar, but she wasn't quite sure why. She tentatively touched it. One eye partially opened and looked at her. The tail wagged weakly.

"Mick?" Melody said, bending closer to look at him. "Mick! It is you!" she cried. She gathered him into her arms, the water from his coat soaking clear through her jacket. He whined and tried to lick her face. "Oh, Mick! What happened to you? Mom, it's Mick. But something bad has happened to him."

Mrs. Morrison knelt beside them and looked at the dog. The once sleek coat was matted and full of burs and other debris. His ribs could be seen under the wet hair, and the pads of his feet were raw, open wounds. Pain and fear dulled his soft brown eyes.

"Can you carry him? Abby's coming. She'll know what to do."

Melody placed her arms under Mick's chest and haunches and picked him up. He couldn't have weighed more than twenty-five pounds, much too light for the size dog he was meant to be. His head rested heavily against her shoulder.

The four-wheel vehicle stopped and Abby ran to them. "What have you got there?" she asked.

"It's Mick. What's happened to him?"

Abby lifted the dog's head and looked in his eyes. "Poor boy," she said softly. "I should never have let you go to with that man." She ran her hand across the protruding ribs and examined the raw pads on his feet. "Let's get him in the truck and take him home," she told Melody.

"What did that man do to him?"

Abby shifted gears and turned the vehicle around, the wheels spinning in the slick mud. "Mick knows how to work sheep, just as long he doesn't get yelled at. In fact, he's very good with sheep because he's not so aggressive that he hurts them." Abby paused. "I told Mr. Lyton that Mick would work as long as he didn't yell at him. He agreed that was okay, so I let Mick go with him. Three weeks ago he called to say Mick ran off when they were driving sheep out of the hills. He had no idea where Mick went or what happened to him. I thought the coyotes might have gotten him."

"He must have been finding his way back home all this time," Mrs. Morrison said. "I've heard of dogs doing that."

"But, why did he run away?" Melody asked.

"Mr. Lyton didn't say, but I suspect Mick didn't understand something or was too slow in carrying out his orders and he yelled at him."

The rain was coming down in windblown torrents by the time they arrived at Abby's house. Melody carried Mick into the spacious kitchen and at Abby's direction laid him on the table . Abby sent her into the bathroom to get out of her wet clothes and put on the terry cloth robe hung behind the door. When Melody returned, she watched while Abby cleaned and bandaged each of Mick's feet and carefully removed the mats and burs from his coat. Abby carefully checked him over for any other injuries. There were some old partially healed cuts, but nothing more serious.

"Put him on the blanket by the stove," she told Melody when she was finished. "I'm going to make up some eggs and milk for him."

"Will he be okay?" Melody asked. She sat beside the dog and stroked his head. She remembered how he greeted her the first day with a paw against her leg and how he followed her everywhere when she was at the ranch. Of all the dogs out here, he had been her favorite. "Will he have to go back?"

"He'll be okay. He's just half starved, but there are no serious injuries, and he doesn't seem to be running a fever, so he's not sick." Abby brought over a bowl with warm milk and egg yolks and set it before Mick. "As for him going back, no. As far as Mr. Lyton is concerned, Mick is dead. He wouldn't want him back anyway because a dog that runs off is no use to him. See if you can get him to drink this. I have some things to go over with your mother."

Mick was too weak to lift his head, so Melody dipped her fingers into the warm mixture and let him lick it off them. "There has to be a faster way than this," she said.

She looked around the kitchen and saw a turkey baster lying on the counter. Melody took it and filled it part way with the milk and egg mixture. She held it so the dog could lick drops from the end. The warm food released quick energy into the emaciated body. By the time he consumed half of it, Mick was able to lift his head enough to lap the rest out of the bowl by himself.

"See, I said he'll be okay," Abby said, coming back to the kitchen in time to see the dog finish the last of the liquid. A weak wag of his tail acknowledged her presence. "Melody, how would you like to have Mick?"

"Have him? You mean for me to keep?"

"I spoke to your mother. It's okay with her if you want him."

Melody looked at the dog who gazed back at her with trusting eyes. "Want him? Yes! Oh, yes, I want him!"

"Then he's yours," Abby said. "I doubt after what happened that he'll ever want to work stock again."

"That's okay," Melody said. "I won't ask him to."

Mick thumped his tail against the floor and whined.

CHAPTER EIGHT:
THE CONTRACT

Melody made a cozy corner for Mick on the enclosed porch off the kitchen. Her mother gave her an old, tattered, but clean quilt, which she folded into a thick, soft bed. Following Abby's instructions, she prepared his food with milk and eggs, gradually adding kibble until he began eating well on his own without coaxing from her. His feet healed rapidly, and within a few days she was able to do away with the bandages. But it was more than a week before he could accompany her on part of her paper route. At first he could walk only part of it, and she had to take him home and put him on the porch. After a couple more weeks he was able to walk the whole distance with her.

From the very first, Melody made friends with practically every dog on her route, including some that never liked paper carriers in the past. She carried small dog biscuits in her pockets to give to each of her canine friends. More importantly, she made friends among her customers. A frequent turnover among carriers had given them poor service for many years. Any special instructions they may have given were often ignored. Melody proved herself not only capable of following instructions, but occasionally improving on those instructions to make getting the paper easier and safer for the more elderly of her customers.

Mick was a perfect companion. He stayed close by Melody's side and never showed jealousy toward the dogs they encountered. Instead, he cowered against Melody if dogs appeared too aggressive. He never barked. He would whine when greeting her after school or if strangers approached them on the street, but that was all. In some ways this was a good thing for a dog living in town, but Melody wondered if he would ever bark as she had heard him do at the ranch when he played with the other dogs or dug for rabbits and gophers.

November dragged on, gray, wet and cold, but never cold enough to freeze the mud out at Abby's. Melody was tired of sloshing through mud puddles, being hit in the face by wet foliage, and having to protect her papers from getting wet. Many times she wanted to just quit the route, but she promised her mother she would keep it until the end of the year. One thing that helped was the thought that as long as the mud remained, Dancer was still at the ranch. And as long as she was there, there was still a chance for a miracle. Many of her older customers remarked how unusual it was for autumn rains to continue as long as they had this year. Melody sometimes wondered if the rain was an answer to her prayers.

The first day of December dawned clear, and ice coated the edges of puddles in the streets. Melody groaned. By the time the weekend arrived, the mud would be frozen and Dancer would be gone.

"We won't be going to the ranch until later this afternoon," Melody's mother said when the girl walked into the kitchen Saturday morning.

"How come?"

"Abby had to go to Seattle this morning and won't be back until late. She asked if we would feed for her. I don't see much sense in going any earlier."

Was that really the reason? Melody wondered. *Maybe Rupert's uncle is going to pick up Dancer today and Abby doesn't want me around.* "I think I'll call Carol," she said.

"After you pick up your room and fold your clean clothes."

"Mom!"

"After," Mrs. Morrison said.

"Oh, okay. Come, Mick," Melody called. Tail wagging, the dog bounded up the stairs ahead of her.

They didn't leave until late afternoon when the sun was about to disappear behind the mountains. Melody was sure Dancer was gone. The last few days had remained well below freezing. She rode with her forehead pressed against the cold window and listlessly watched the brown winter landscape go by. She had wanted to stay home, but her mother insisted that she come along, saying she needed her help.

Melody didn't bother looking in Dancer's stall as she walked past it to get the wheelbarrow and manure fork. She heard an indignant nicker and a rough shove against her shoulder nearly knocked her down.

"Dancer!" she cried, turning back. "You're still here!" Melody threw her arms around the filly's neck and buried her face in the tousled mane. She breathed deeply of the scent that belonged only to this horse. Her mother laughed the time she told her about being able to tell by smell alone which horse was Dancer. "Why are you still here?" Melody asked. *Did someone change his mind? Or did he forget? Fat chance that happened. Well, no matter the reason, I have one more time with my favorite horse.*

Before hay and grain had been given to all the horses and their water buckets de-iced and refilled, the remaining daylight disappeared, leaving behind a clear, moonless December night. The north wind, which had been blowing all day, increased and drove cold air through Melody's down jacket.

"I'm going in the house to warm up," Mrs. Morrison said as she approached Melody, who was brushing the red dun filly in the stall. "Are you coming?"

"I want to stay a while longer with Dancer. I'll be in after a bit."

"Just don't get too cold."

Melody spent longer than usual currying and brushing Dancer's red-gold coat and combing the tangles out of her mane and tail, all the time trying not to think this could be the last time she would be able to do this.. Several of the long red tail strands pulled out, and these Melody carefully wound into a loose circle and stuck in her pocket. She planned to make a bracelet out of them. At least she would be able to call that much of Dancer her own. Only when her toes began to lose feeling did she pet the horse's neck one last time and go to the house.

Welcome warmth greeted Melody as she walked through the back door. Her mother handed her a cup of hot chocolate. The heat from the ceramic mug felt good as she clutched it in both hands. "Are we leaving soon?" she asked.

"Abby called and asked us to wait for her to get back."

"How long will that be?"

"She was calling from the pass. Probably another hour."

Melody went into the living room and sat on the thick tan carpet. Mick snuggled next to her and laid his head in her lap. She took the strands of tail hair and began knotting them into a flat band. Carol had shown her that afternoon how to make a friendship bracelet using colored cording. It had been easy with the cord, but Melody found the hair was slippery. She had trouble controlling the knots; and if she pulled too hard, the hair would break.

Melody was so engrossed in her handiwork she didn't notice the passage of time. She looked up at the clock and was surprised an hour and a half had passed. "How much longer do we have to wait?" she asked.

Mrs. Morrison glanced at her watch. "We'll give her a little more time."

Another half hour passed. Melody finished the bracelet and tied it around her ankle. Her mother got up and went into the kitchen. Melody followed and saw her take a covered dish out of the refrigerator.

"What are you doing?" she asked.

"Thought I'd heat up some of this stew Abby left. She told me to go ahead and use it if she was delayed."

"Why don't we just go home?"

"Because I promised her we'd stay until she got back." Mrs. Morrison emptied the thick brown stew into a heavy pan and set it on a burner.

"Mom, is there something going on I should know about?" Melody asked.

"Why do you ask?"

"Oh, I don't know. It just seems strange that Abby wants us to wait for her. She's been gone from the ranch before and never asked us to stay."

"She has her reasons, I'm sure."

The rich, meaty aroma of the stew filled the kitchen and the window over the stove steamed up. Melody realized she was hungrier than she thought. She and her mother were cleaning their bowls with slices of Abby's homemade bread when headlights shone through the window.

"Melody, why don't you clean up while I talk with Abby," Mrs. Morrison said. She went to meet the ranch owner at the door.

"What about the rest of the stew?"

"Leave it out," Abby said, coming into the house and shedding her thickly padded jacket. "I'm hungry, but first I want to talk with your mother alone."

Melody cleared the used dishes from the table and put on a clean setting for Abby. She ran hot water in the sink and washed what she and her mother used, plus the few items Abby left on the counter that morning. She heard the droning of the two women talking in the next room, but couldn't make out any of the words. She was wiping the stove top when they called her name.

There was something strange about the way her mother and Abby were standing and waiting for her. Melody couldn't quite figure it out, but she knew something was going on.

"I want you to read this," Mrs. Morrison said. She handed two sheets of paper to Melody.

"Contract for Sale," in bold letters was printed across the top of the first page. Melody blinked. She continued reading, "For the sum of Two Thousand Four Hundred Dollars, Abigail Jankins agrees to sell the red dun American Quarter Horse named Dont Skippa Dance to Melody Morrison, under the following conditions."

Melody stopped reading and sat down on the edge of the sofa.

Surely her eyes were playing tricks on her, she thought. She read
the beginning again, and looked up at her mother and Abby. Both
of them were grinning like a couple of teenagers. "Is this really
true?" she asked. Both women nodded. "But - but how . . ."

"I could see how you and Dancer belonged to each other,"
Abby said. "I guess I saw it the very first day." She sat next to
Melody. "Anyway, it bothered me that a man like Roland Farrady
wanted a horse like Dancer. He's not a horse person. So I did some
checking around and learned he planned to sell her to people in
California who have more money than they do horse sense. Anyway, to make a long story short, I called my son in Seattle and
asked if he could help. I was over there today to get the money
from him, and tonight I paid Roland the money that was owed
him."

"I can really buy her? This is really happening?"

"Yes," Abby said. "You can buy Dancer."

Melody shook her head. She looked at her mother. "Mom,
this is real? It's not a dream?"

Mrs. Morrison laughed. "No, it's not a dream. In little more
than a year's time she'll be all yours if you make the payments as
stated."

Melody looked at the contract again. She felt the paper between her fingers to be sure it existed.

"There are some conditions listed there that you should know
about," Mrs. Morrison said. "You'll have to keep Dancer here at
Abby's until she's paid for in full. You'll be responsible to pay for
her feed, shoeing costs, vet bills, and anything else that comes up.
And you have to keep the payments up or you will forfeit her back
to Abby. Think you'll be able to do that?"

Melody did some quick calculations in her head. She looked
at the contract to see what the payments would be. Yes, there
would be enough from the paper route to make the payments and
still have a little left over. "I can do it," she said quietly.

"I won't charge you for her stall until she's paid off," Abby
added. "Well, do you still want to buy her?"

"Yes!" Melody shouted. "Oh, yes!" Her eyes misted, but with happy tears. "Thank you. Thank you," she said, hugging first Abby, then her mother.

"Okay. Then you and your mother and I will sign this contract," Abby said. "This is only to protect us all from any misunderstandings in the future."

"Mom, is that okay with you?"

Mrs. Morrison nodded. "Who do you think helped draw this up in the first place?"

"You knew it all the time, and you didn't say anything?"

"Believe me, it was awfully hard not to. You're not an easy one to keep a secret from."

The line on the page was a blur. Melody's hand shook so much she could hardly sign her name. She dropped the pen, grabbed her coat, and ran out the door. She heard her mother and Abby laughing in the house as she raced for the barn.

CHAPTER NINE:
WILD DOGS

"How are you coming with buying that horse?" Mrs. Nenana asked when Melody stopped to collect the monthly paper payment.

"She's one-quarter mine already," Melody replied, smiling. She handed change back to the elderly woman. The once cantankerous Mrs. Nenana. had become one of Melody's staunchest supporters over the last few months. Once she found out why Melody was doing the route, she never failed to inquire about the horse or how Melody herself was doing.

"Well, good luck to you, child. That's an awfully big responsibility."

"But she's worth it," Melody said.

The old woman took some of the bills out of the money Melody gave back to her. "Maybe this will help a little," she said, putting it in the girl's hand.

"It will. Thanks. See you next month. Come, Mick."

The black-and-white Border Collie followed her down the snow-covered walk. His coat was thick and shiny again, and almost too much flesh covered his ribs now. His eyes were once again soft and not fearful, and his tail had a jaunty wag. Every line in his body showed he adored Melody; but she wasn't sure if he would protect her if she ever needed it. Mick was still very much a coward.

Ever since she signed the contract for Dancer, Melody did the route with a light heart. Every penny she earned went toward Dancer's payments and support; she spent none on herself. Whatever was left over, she placed in a special basket up in her room.

This was her fund for use in emergencies if any should come up. Each month there seemed to be quite a sum to put in the basket because of generous tips her customers gave her. In addition, she developed such a good reputation for delivering papers on time and putting them where customers wanted, that several new accounts were added to her route. Between the increased income and the tips, Melody figured she might be able to pay off Dancer a full month or two ahead of schedule if nothing unforeseen happened.

Winter was unusually dry after the heavy autumn rains. The lack of snow made it easy for Melody to deliver her papers, and for her and her mother to get to the ranch on Saturdays. However, Abby and other ranchers in the area were concerned there might not be enough snow in the mountains for irrigation water in the summer.

Melody continued her lessons on Miss Piggy on Saturdays when the wind wasn't blowing too hard. She was becoming a very good rider under Abby's tutelage. They began working on the finer points of good western pleasure riding.

"How would you like to show?" Abby asked her one day.

"I don't know. I'm not that good yet."

"Oh, I don't know about that. I think you're doing quite well. You've got a good seat and a natural way about you."

"Where are there shows I could enter? I don't want to have to join the horse club—those people are a bunch of snobs, especially Jean Monroe." Earlier in the year Melody had asked around about 4-H or other clubs that she might join so she could learn more about horses. Most of the kids were into raising pigs, sheep or cattle. Only one club dealt with horses, and Jean belonged to it.

"There's an open show in October at the Fair Grounds," Abby said. "That means anyone can enter. It's not just for members of the horse club. Think about it."

"Would Dancer be ready by then? I'd really like to ride her if I can."

"Possibly. There's a Green Horse Class for horses under saddle less than a year. She might be ready. We'll be starting her with the saddle in a couple of weeks if this weather holds."

Melody smiled. "Then let's work on getting her ready for that class."

Melody soon discovered there was a lot of work to do around a ranch after winter. Abby showed her how to check fencing around the pastures. She learned how to mend places where the wire had broken and how to pound in metal posts to replace rotted wooden ones. Melody caught on quickly. Soon she was allowed to ride Miss Piggy by herself out into the fields and repair fences wherever they needed it. Mick, ever faithful, trotted beside them or made nearby side excursions to chase a meadow lark or rabbit. Still he didn't bark.

"When you go out today," Abby said one Saturday toward the end of March, "keep a lookout for a pack of stray dogs. They've been chasing stock in these areas."

"Where did they come from?" Melody asked. She tightened the cinch on the saddle and checked to see that it sat properly on Miss Piggy's back.

"City folks who move out here think the country's a great place to let their dogs run free. And others who get tired of their pets, turn them loose, thinking they can fend for themselves. Trouble is, when a group of these dogs get together, they become no better than a wild pack and will chase anything. They can't catch the wild deer or elk, but they can catch domestic stock." Abby looked sternly at Melody. "If you see them, don't try making friends with them. I know you love dogs, but these animals forget their domestic training when they get into a pack like that."

"What do you want me to do if I see them?" Melody asked as she swung easily into the saddle.

"High tail it back here as fast as you can," Abby said. "Miss Piggy still has enough speed to outrun them. We'll get Animal Control out here if they show up."

A light breeze was blowing as Melody headed to the far side of Abby's ranch. The air was still cool from the snow pack in the mountains, but the spring sun was warm. She noticed male red-winged blackbirds staking out their territories in the dried reeds still standing from last year. Green shoots of new cattails were poking their heads above the water they grew in. Melody remembered her mother telling her once those tender shoots were supposed to be good eating, but she had never mustered the courage to try them. In the next pasture, Melody saw Dancer and several other horses grazing on the new spring grass. Two of the horses were heavy with foal, and Melody could hardly wait to see the babies.

A large section of fence at the very back of the property had broken down during the winter. Deer and elk pushing through in their search for food had snapped the old and brittle wire, and some of the clips holding the strands to the metal posts had fallen off. Melody dismounted and took her fencing tool out of the saddle bag. When Abby gave her the strange implement as a birthday present, she didn't realize how useful it could be. Hinged like a pair of pliers, one side had a flattened head that could be used like a hammer, and the other had a point which was useful in getting under wire staples to pull them out or for picking stones out of a horse's hoof. The end where the two sides came together could be used in the same manner as a pair pliers. The sides of the hinge toward the handles were notched to form wire cutters of two different sizes and of considerable cutting ability. Melody became quite adept using this tool while working with Abby.

Miss Piggy lowered her head and grazed while Melody worked. She had to use much of the spare wire she brought in order to splice together broken ends. The fence at this end of the property was in extremely poor condition. Abby was going to have to replace it with all new posts and wire one of these days soon. She was fastening the last strand to a post when she heard the sound of pounding hooves.

Mick barked.

Melody looked in the direction he was facing. She caught her breath. The horses, Dancer among them, were being chased by a pack of five or six dogs of varying sizes and colors. The leader was a wolfish looking cross of some kind. They were chasing the horses straight for the fence that separated the fields.

Throwing her tool into the saddle bag, Melody gathered Miss Piggy's reins and mounted in one quick motion. Meanwhile, Mick ran toward the horses and pack of dogs, barking furiously.

"Mick!" Melody screamed. He didn't stop. He never looked back. *He's not running away*, Melody noticed. *No, he's going directly toward the commotion. Was he joining the pack? Not Mick!*

As one of the species on the food list for predators, a horse's first instinct is to run when attacked. Even Dancer, who was used to having dogs around, panicked when the pack appeared and fled with the rest of the herd. The horses continued straight for the fence. Melody watched, horrified, as they ran through it, breaking the wire. All of them seemed to make it okay. Then Dancer pitched forward and fell. The dogs surrounded her.

"No!" Melody screamed, and she kicked Miss Piggy into a run. "Get away from her!" she yelled.

Dancer struggled to her feet and tried to get away, but wire was wrapped around her leg and held her. A red streak ran down the leg. She turned to face her attackers. She whinnied long and loud.

Melody was still several hundred feet away when a black and white blur rushed the nearest dog to Dancer. Mick struck the dog with his chest, knocking it over. He flashed away before it could turn on him. He rushed another dog twice his size, slashed at it with bared teeth, and dashed away again. He whirled, seemingly in all directions at once, throwing the pack into confusion. Melody had never seen him move so fast. The dogs withdrew their attention from Dancer and turned toward Mick. The leader's teeth connected on Mick's shoulder. Melody heard him yelp.

"Mick! Get out of there!" she screamed.

She didn't know if he heard her or even if he understood her command, but Mick broke off his attack and ran. The majority of the pack went after him. He ran away from Dancer and Melody and toward the hills.

Tears poured from Melody's eyes as she dismounted by Dancer. Two dogs lurked a short distance away. She picked up several rocks and threw them at the dogs. She hit one of them, a scarred tan and black, and it ran off yelping. Melody looked for Mick, but he had disappeared into the trees. She could hear the pack barking as they followed him. "Oh, Lord, please help Mick be okay," she prayed. Then she looked at Dancer.

The wire was twisted tightly around her rear leg and cut deeply into the bend of the hock. Flesh had been stripped down to a white substance that looked like bone to Melody. A flap of bloody tissue hung below the wound. Dancer stood quietly once the dogs were gone, and continued to do so while the girl took her fencing tool and cut the wire from around the leg. Limping, Dancer took a few steps forward.

Melody examined the injured leg. She had never seen anything so ugly. Something was needed to bind it before she could lead Dancer back to the barn. She looked down at what she was wearing. Under her jacket was her favorite sweatshirt with the picture of a horse Dancer's color. Mom gave it to her just a couple of weeks ago for her fourteenth birthday. The material was thick and soft and still clean. Shucking her jacket, she took the shirt off and put her jacket back on. With the help of a pocket knife, she tore the shirt into several strips. She brought the flap of flesh back up over the wound and bandaged the leg with the remains of her sweatshirt. Once the wound was covered, Melody took one of Miss Piggy's reins from her bridle and tied it loosely around Dancer's neck. Leading a horse with each hand, Melody began the long walk back to the barn.

CHAPTER TEN: FIRST RIDE

"How bad is it?" Melody asked Dr. Stickles as he cleaned the wound on Dancer's leg. She winched when he cut the loose flap of skin and flesh away, leaving a large, raw hole in the leg. "Will she be lame?"

The ruddy complexioned man straightened and looked at her. "It's bad," he said, "but with proper care it will heal with barely a scar. And no, she won't be lame."

"But didn't it cut her to the bone?"

"Why do you think that?"

"That white stuff there."

The veterinarian chuckled. "That was tendon, not bone, you see. Fortunately, it was only laid bare, not cut." He took a spray bottle from his array of supplies, and squirted a brown liquid on the wound. A strong odor, that was quite different from any medicine she ever smelled before, reached Melody's nose. "I'm going to show you how to clean and bandage this, young lady. You watch, too, Abby."

The older woman moved next to Melody. The doctor took a yellow ball that looked like it was made out of plastic string out of one of the compartments.

"Why, it looks just like the scrubby thing we use in the kitchen at home!" Melody said. "You don't mean for us to use that on her, do you?"

Dr. Stickles grinned. "Not right away, but in a few days when the proud flesh begins forming."

"What's proud flesh?"

"You see, a wound like this can't be stitched and closed up.

That leaves a wide area the body needs to fill in with new flesh. So a blood-rich granular tissue forms at the edges and grows toward the middle until the injured area is covered. Left to itself, this granular flesh will produce far more than what the body needs, thus causing an unsightly thick scar to form. What you will do once the excess flesh begins forming is to scrub it away with this thing." He indicated the plastic scrub ball.

"But, won't it hurt her?" Melody protested.

"I suppose it does somewhat, but most horses seem to handle it quite well. Remember, you are only scrubbing away the excess flesh, not that which is closing in the wound and beginning to form new skin. Abby, you know what I'm talking about."

Abby nodded. "I've done this before, Mel. It's not as hard as it sounds."

"Can a hole that big really heal without a scar?" Melody asked. The gaping hole in Dancer's leg was almost as big as her fist.

"It can," the doctor said. "You'll be surprised at the regenerative powers a healthy body has. Plus, we'll be giving it a little help." He handed her the bottle of strange smelling brown liquid he had squirted on the wound.

"What's this stuff?" she asked.

"Something I discovered a couple of years ago. It's made with healing herbs. Works better than anything I've ever used manufactured by the pharmaceutical houses, especially on wire cuts like this." He finished wrapping a bright blue elasticized bandage around Dancer's leg. He went to his truck and took a small book from the cab. "Take a look at these," he said, handing the book to Melody.

She opened it and saw several pictures of a horse with both back legs cut as badly as Dancer's.

"I treated a similar case last year. I took these pictures when the owner was doubtful about anything natural being used. I made a deal with him—one leg I'd treat the conventional way, the other with this liquid. The pictures on the left show the traditional way of treatment."

Melody and Abby looked at the photos together. Dates in the lower right hand corners indicated they had been taken every two days during treatment. The first one or two sets of pictures didn't show any great difference; but by the time they got to the fourth set, Melody pointed to the leg on the right. "Look, Abby."

"I see."

"It's pretty amazing stuff," Dr. Stickles said. "Twelve days into treatment the owner was begging me to start treating the other leg with this stuff. Take a look at the last picture."

The last photo showed both legs completely healed, but the one first treated by conventional means showed a noticeable scar. The other leg showed barely a trace of injury.

"Will Dancer's leg heal like that?" Melody asked.

"It should. Just remember to do as I told you."

Melody led Dancer to her stall. She looked at the bandaged leg and thought how close she came to losing her horse to those dogs. If it hadn't been for Mick . . . Mick! He risked his life to keep the dogs off Dancer, and now he was somewhere out in the hills running for his own life from a pack of vicious dogs.

"Abby, we've got to go look for Mick."

The woman shook her head. "If he's in the hills, we won't find him before dark. Animal Control is already sending someone out looking for that pack."

"But, they'll think Mick is one of them!"

"I told them the only black and white dog in that group didn't belong with the pack. They assured me they wouldn't shoot him."

"He saved Dancer, you know."

"I know."

Melody didn't sleep that night, and once the papers were delivered the next morning, she wanted to go straight out to the ranch instead of to church. In spite of her and her mother's protests, her father insisted they attend Sunday service as usual.

"If he's not there," he said, "there's nothing you can do. If he's there, Abby will take care of him. Now I'll hear no more about it."

Normally, Melody enjoyed the singing and worship, but all

she could think about was Mick and what might be happening to him. She knew he could run fast, faster than any of the other dogs at the ranch. She hoped that speed kept him away from the pack.

The singing ended. "Before we go to prayer," the pastor said, "does anyone have a request?"

Several hands went up, Melody's among them. He nodded to her.

"Pray for my dog, Mick," she said, struggling to keep her voice from breaking. "He saved my horse from a pack of dogs yesterday. They were chasing him into the hills the last time I saw him."

A snicker came from the back of the church.

The pastor held up his hand and shook his head. "There's nothing wrong in asking God to help the animals we love," he said. "They are living, breathing beings, and God cares for them, too. We'll remember Mick, Melody. Anyone else have a request?"

Prayer was asked for the usual illnesses and travel safety, and a couple of people gave reports of prayers being answered. The pastor began the prayer and several members of the congregation took turns praying for one or more of the several spoken petitions or those listed in the bulletin. Tears ran freely down Melody's cheeks when an elderly man prayed specifically for Mick's safety, asking God to protect him as he had protected Melody and her horse.

Immediately after church, Melody and her mother drove to the ranch. Melody's eyes searched the sage covered hills. She wondered if Mick was up there somewhere, perhaps torn by the dog pack, or lost and scared. She was sorry she ever thought of him as a coward. When he sensed danger to something he felt responsible for, he acted with no thought for his own safety.

Abby was waiting when they drove into the yard. "I have something you'll want to see," she said. "Go down and look in Dancer's stall."

Melody sprang out of the car, leaving the door open behind her, and raced for the barn. Almost not daring to breathe, she peered over the half door into the darkened stall. Dancer turned her head when she saw Melody, but she didn't move from where she was standing. Instead, the horse looked down at something by her feet. Melody's heart skipped a beat. A black and white bundle of hair was curled in the straw.

"Mick?" she said tentatively. Opening the stall door, she slipped in and knelt. "Mick?"

A sleepy eye opened and gazed at her. He reached up and licked her hand, and rolled over for her to rub his belly.

"Oh, Mick! You wonderful, crazy, silly dog!" Melody cried, gathering him in her arms and hugging him. His long pink tongue washed tears from her face.

"He's pretty tired," Abby said. "He came limping in about eleven-thirty this morning. His pads are raw and he's got a couple of superficial bite wounds, but other than that he seems okay."

"How come he's here in Dancer's stall?"

"That's a funny thing. After I fed him, he begged to go in there. I figured he knew what he wanted, and Dancer certainly doesn't mind. She's been standing guard over him ever since."

"My two favorite animals," Melody said, wiping her eyes. "You said he came in about eleven-thirty?"

"About that."

Melody looked up at her mother and they both smiled. "That's when special prayer was said for him in church," she told Abby.

By the time spring burst forth in full floral regalia, the wound on Dancer's leg had closed up and hair began covering the new skin. To both Melody's and Abby's relief, Dancer never showed signs of lameness. Animal Control hunted down and shot or trapped the dog pack. Two of them still wore collars and tags, enabling authorities to find their owners. Heavy fines were levied against the men for not having their dogs under control, and they were court ordered to pay restitution to people who had livestock killed or injured by the pack. Melody received a small sum of money which was sufficient to pay most of Dancer's vet bills so she didn't have to use all of her emergency fund.

Two mares, one of them Dancer's mother, had their long-legged foals. Dancer's little brother looked almost exactly like his sister, right down to the two white legs in back and two white feet in the front and a broad white blaze. He also loved attention as much as Dancer did.

Early in May, Abby announced, "I think it's time Dancer felt a rider on her back."

"Do you think she'll buck?"

"If we've done our ground work right, she shouldn't. She didn't buck when we put the saddle on her the first time. And she didn't seem to mind weight being put in the stirrups."

"Who's going to get on first?" Melody asked.

"That will be me," Abby replied. "You've become quite good as a rider, but you've not ridden any horse but Miss Piggy. A young horse can be unpredictable at times. And the last thing you want to do is confuse her by giving her the wrong signals if something starts to go wrong."

Melody hoped to be the first to sit on Dancer's back, but she had to admit Abby's reasoning made a lot of sense. She knew they both spent lots of hours with the filly, accustoming her to the saddle and bridle and other equipment commonly used around horses. They had desensitized her by drawing various things like blankets and bags across her head and between her legs so she wouldn't spook if the wind blew something against her or a dog ran between her feet. Abby believed in a solid foundation being laid before a rider ever sat on a horse's back. She said that was the best way to develop a safe horse, one that trusted its rider and wouldn't react out of fear when something unusual happened.

Dancer stood still while Melody saddled her. Her introduction to the heavy leather contraption had been one step at a time. She knew it was nothing to be afraid of. However, she still curled her lip and made funny faces when the metal bit first touched her closed teeth. By placing her thumb in the corner of Dancer's mouth, Melody made the filly open her mouth. She slipped the bit behind the front incisors and let it lie in the toothless area of the jaw before the molars.

Melody led the horse to the round pen. The loose sand would

give less traction for Dancer's feet. If Abby should be bucked off, the landing would be softer than the harder arena surface.

Abby did a quick check of the tack and nodded approvingly when she saw Melody had fastened everything properly. She took the filly to the center of the pen and placed her left foot in the stirrup. Dancer twisted her head around and looked at her. Abby put some weight in the stirrup. Dancer stood still. With one smooth, easy movement, Abby pulled herself up, balanced over the saddle, swung her leg over the horse's rump and sat in the saddle.

Still Dancer didn't move except for a twitching of her ears. The woman squeezed her legs gently and clucked to the horse. The squeeze was something new, but Dancer knew well the cluck. She moved forward at a steady walk. Abby tightened the right rein slightly. Dancer turned to the right. Abby tightened the left rein. Dancer turned to the left. She pulled back lightly on both reins and sat back in the saddle. Dancer stopped. Grinning, Abby dismounted.

"I'll do more work with her tomorrow," she said, handing the reins to Melody. "She responds beautifully. I don't think we're going to have any trouble with her."

"Then why are you stopping so soon?" Melody asked.

"It's best to leave a training session on a good note," Abby explained. "That may not always be possible; but if you can let your horse feel it's done a good job, it will be eager to learn the next time."

"Like people," Melody reflected. "I always like doing my best whenever someone tells me I'm doing a good job."

By the time Abby rode Dancer the third time that week, she knew the horse was trustworthy enough for Melody to try. That Saturday, she told Melody to get on the red dun. Trembling with excitement, Melody mounted the horse that was now one-third hers. Dancer nickered when she saw who was on her. Melody squeezed her legs, and the filly stepped forward. She moved so smoothly! Just like she looked from the ground. Melody guided her in different directions. Each time Dancer did exactly what her rider wanted.

"Get her to jog," Abby ordered.

Melody squeezed her legs a little more and made a kissing sound. Dancer moved into the slow, ground eating gait. What a pleasure! The jog had been teeth-rattling rough on Miss Piggy, but on Dancer it was almost like sitting in a rocking chair. Melody relaxed. She felt she could go on forever like this.

"I think you'll be ready for the green horse class by October," Abby said. "Yup. I do believe you two were definitely meant for each other."

CHAPTER ELEVEN: COW PIES

"Mel, the cows are in the lower hay field. Take Dancer and go put them back."

Melody looked up from cleaning mud out of Miss Piggy's feet. "Which saddle should I use?"

"You'll have to use the show saddle," Abby said after a moment's thought. "I haven't had a chance to get the stirrup fixed on the cutter yet."

"Are you sure?" Melody asked. The show saddle was decorated with real silver conchos and was one of the few personal things Abby had left from her late husband. It was never used for working cattle.

"It'll be okay. Now get going."

The show saddle was considerably heavier than the cutting saddle, but months of working at the ranch had strengthened Melody's arms. She swung it easily up on Dancer's back. While she adjusted the blanket and made sure the saddle sat properly, the filly nuzzled her back pocket. There were no pieces of carrot or apple this time. Annoyed, Dancer bumped Melody's backside with her nose.

"You should have been named Miss Piggy," Melody laughed. She threw her arms around the red dun's neck and buried her face in the unruly mane, loving the warm horsey smell. She found it hard to believe Dancer was nearly half hers now. Not to be left out, Mick placed a paw against Melody's leg. The girl reached down and ruffled his ears.

"I'm so lucky," she said, "to have two such wonderful friends as you." Mick licked her hand while Dancer snuffled in her ear.

The previous night's rain made everything sparkling and green in the early morning sun. Dancer pranced a few steps into the lane leading to the lower pasture. The cool air made her want to run, but Melody held her down to a walk. Mick, being under no such restraint, ranged out into the field, sniffing out the trail of a rabbit or ground squirrel.

Relaxed, Melody's lithe body moved in rhythm with Dancer's motion. The horse and rider appeared as one being. Sitting on a horse seemed the most natural thing in the world to Melody. She wondered if all the hours she spent on her Wonder Horse® as a baby had anything to do with that.

Tall grasses bordered the lane, occasionally broken by clumps of wild roses full of pink blossoms with yellow halos for centers. Bees worked industriously among the flowers, gathering nectar and pollen for the lean winter months. A killdeer darted across the lane, faking a broken wing. Melody knew if she dismounted and looked carefully, she would find its chicks crouched motionless in a clump of grass nearby. Overhead a circling red-tail hawk screamed its hunting cry.

This was living, Melody thought. This was what she was born to do. People could have the city if they wanted it. The constant noise of traffic, the garbage-littered streets in the downtown area, and the stench of diesel and asphalt under a hot summer sun had assaulted her senses when they lived in Seattle.

There was a gate at the end of the lane. Melody sidled Dancer up to it. She had to lean way over so she could reach the lever. The procedure was easy on Miss Piggy, who was a whole two hands, or eight inches, shorter. Holding the saddle horn, Melody placed all her weight in the left stirrup and reached for the gate handle. At that particular moment, Dancer decided she had been standing still long enough. She took a couple of steps forward. Melody found herself suspended between the saddle and the gate.

"Oh, sh . . .!" Melody stopped short of saying the whole word. "Dancer, get back here!" she yelled.

The horse turned her head and fixed a puzzled look on her rider.

This was a new experience, and she didn't quite know what to do about it. She tried to get a better look by turning her body. This made her move farther from the gate.

Melody felt her grip on both the gate handle and the saddle horn slip. She gave up trying to open the gate and grabbed for the saddle. Her center of gravity was too far to one side. She missed the horn and fell with a loud, "Ummph!" Dancer looked down at her with a "what are you doing down there?" expression. Mick appeared out of the tall grass and began licking her face. In spite of pain where her hip hit a rock, Melody giggled.

"At least no one was around to see this," she said to Dancer and Mick. She pulled herself up by the stirrup and gently felt the side of her thigh. Yup, there was going to be another bruise to add to her growing collection.

As she turned toward the pasture, she saw the place the cows had broken through. The electric fence wire sagged during the heavy rain, shorting out on the wet grass. Although plenty of succulent grass grew on their own side of the fence, the field of orchard grass and alfalfa being grown for hay looked far more inviting. Before riding from the barn, Melody remembered to turn off the power to the fence so she knew there was no danger of her being shocked. She moved the wire out of the way. And rode Dancer through the opening. Mick slipped away on business of his own.

Their bellies full, the whole herd was lying down and chewing cuds. They watched with mild curiosity as horse and rider approached. Melody took off her hat and began waving it and shouting, "Ho, cows! Get up there!"

Her words didn't mean a thing to the bovines, but the rider circling behind them and the waving hat did. One by one the cows and calves hiked their rear ends up and scrambled to their feet. They ambled toward the lowered section of fence, except for one little spotted shorthorn bull calf. He decided he wanted to stay in the hay field. He turned, and before Melody could guide Dancer to cut him off, he zig zagged his way past the girl and her horse and ran behind them into the open field.

The calf was fast, but Dancer's long legs gave her an advantage. She circled ahead of the runaway. With a little guidance from Melody, she started driving it back. The herd was now making its way back to their own pasture through the opening in the fence. The calf followed them.

Melody prepared to dismount to mend the wire. The spotted calf realized he wasn't where he wanted to be. He whirled around and darted past Melody and Dancer. Once again horse and rider took off after him.

The heavy rain the night before left the grass too wet for the sun to have dried it yet. In addition, the cows had spent several hours in the hay field. Dancer ran full bore after the troublesome calf. Her feet hit a saturated section of grass liberally dotted with the cows' leavings. At that same second she turned to follow the calf as he changed directions. All four feet lost their traction and slid out from under her. The momentum threw Melody from the saddle. She went sliding head first through the soggy grass and green, slimy manure.

For a few moments both horse and rider lay where they landed. Melody was first to get up. She looked at the greenish brown goo that coated her from her chin to her boot tops.

"Oh, yuck!" She tried shaking the stuff off her hands. It stuck like glue.

Melody looked around. She saw Dancer lying where she had fallen a short distance away. The horse was lying still—too still. Melody's heart skipped a beat. "Nooooo!" she screamed. "Dancer, get up! You've got to be okay! You just have to be!"

Tears ran down Melody's face. She ran the few yards between her and the motionless horse. But before she reached the filly, Dancer rolled over, sat up, and clambered to her feet. Cow manure covered her from neck to rump. But there was not one speck on the show saddle.

Dancer sniffed in Melody's direction and curled her nose at the scent.

"Well, you don't smell any better yourself," Melody said.

She threw her arms around the horse's neck and hugged her, not caring that she was smearing the manure thoroughly on both of them.

Stepping back, Melody looked the horse over, then down at herself. The full impact of the sight they presented suddenly hit her. She started to laugh, just a small giggle at first. Once started, though, she couldn't stop. Soon she was holding her sides and gasping for breath, and still laughter came. Dancer stood looking at her quizzically for a few moments, then dropped her head to snatch a few mouthfuls of grass.

Melody ran out of breath. She looked around to find the wayward calf. It was nonchalantly drinking from its mother's udder over on the right side of the fence. Mick was lying in the grass by the downed wire, a happy doggie grin on his face.

Melody led Dancer through the opening in the fence. She wiped her hands somewhat clean on a patch of grass and spliced the ends of the wire together. With Mick proudly trotting by her side, she led Dancer back to the barn. She could have ridden, but she didn't feel like cleaning cow manure out of the intricately hammered silver work decorating the saddle.

CHAPTER TWELVE:
SHOW DAY

"Carol, Dancer is so smooth!" Melody bubbled as the girls walked into school the first day after summer vacation. The girls hadn't seen one another for several weeks. "I can't believe what a dream she is to ride!"

"Probably because she's just an old plow horse."

Melody looked around and saw Jean walking behind them. "She's not a plow horse!" she retorted.

"Well, whatever," Jean said, flipping golden curls back from her face. "Bet she couldn't compete against a REAL horse."

Heat rose in Melody's face. "What do you mean?"

"She couldn't win anything in a horse show, dummy."

"We'll see. I'm entering her in the Green Horse Class at the open show."

Jean snorted. "Then I know you won't win anything. My Arab is going to outdo her. My dad paid over fifteen thousand for him. And, I've got a famous trainer working with me."

"What a snob!" Melody said when Jean left to join a group of her friends. "Where does she get off talking that way?"

"Don't pay any attention to her," Carol said. "She equates money with being better. You haven't seen her horse."

"Have you?"

"From a distance. He's pretty, a sort of silvery color. But he looks like he'd be a handful. Didn't you tell me the Green Horse Class was supposed to show how safe and responsive a young horse can be?"

Melody nodded. "Abby said half of the judging is on the behavior of the horse; the other half is on the skill of the rider."

"There you are. From what you've told me, Dancer will literally walk circles around Jean's Arab while he prances her into third place."

Melody giggled at the thought of Jean's expression if that ever happened.

The weeks before the open show seemed far too short. Abby helped Melody refine her riding techniques, and Melody worked on Dancer's appearance. She clipped long hairs to make the horse's muzzle and ears smooth and neat. She worked bottles of conditioner into the long tail and mane hairs and carefully combed out all the tangles. The tail behaved beautifully, but the mane seemed to have a mind of its own. No matter what Melody did, there was one section about one third the way up the filly's neck which absolutely refused to lie flat.

"Abby, what are we going to do? We can't let her go into the ring looking like this!" Melody pressed the offending section of mane down , only to have it pop straight up once she removed her hand.

"I think you are going to get some of the strongest hair spray you can find."

"Hair spray? You mean the kind people use?"

"Sure. Why not? You use it to hold your hair in place, don't you?"

Melody nodded. Well, it might work, she thought. The horse shampoo did a good job getting both her and Dancer clean after the cow pies, so maybe people stuff would work on horses, too.

Five o'clock show day morning came too soon for Melody. She spent most of the night unable to sleep, and by the time she finally drifted off, the alarm rang.

"No breakfast for me today, Mom."

"But you've got to eat something."

"I can't."

"Okay. Maybe later."

"Mom, do you think Dad will be back in time?"

Mrs. Morrison shrugged her shoulders. "He said he'd try to. I'm sure he'll make it if he can."

By the time Melody and her mother arrived at the ranch, Abby already had the horse trailer hitched up. Together they checked the tack and grooming supplies to be sure nothing was overlooked. Dancer wore a light weight blanket to keep her clean. Melody looked at the horse with pride. *Almost two-thirds mine,* she thought. *Some people, including Dad, don't believe kids my age can stick to a commitment like this. But Mom has never lost faith in me.* Melody looked at her mother and smiled. "Thanks, Mom," she said.

"You're welcome, but I don't know what you're thanking me for."

"For believing in me," Melody replied.

Trucks and horse trailers filled nearly all available parking spots by the time Abby drove her rig into the fair grounds. They were forced to find a place way in the back, a good city block away from the show pavilion. Melody saw Jean a couple of rows over. She was grooming a silver-gray Arabian gelding. Melody had to admit, the horse was pretty, but he did seem high strung.

"You better go get your number," Abby told Melody. "We'll take care of Dancer."

Her mother handed her the entry fee. "Get a good number," she said.

A number of contestants were crowded around the show secretary's table. Jean Monroe and a group of girls Melody didn't know were standing in a cluster to one side, each holding a red-and-white card. They looked her way, and she heard them laugh and say something among themselves. Melody tried to ignore them. She turned toward the table and handed her money to the woman. She received a red card with a white eighty-seven emblazoned on it, along with a safety pin for attaching it to the back of her shirt.

"Hey, Melody," Jean called in a syrupy sweet tone, "what number did you get?"

"Eighty-seven."

Jean held her placard up. Three one's stood in a neat row across it. "Look at this and know I'm going to beat you in the ring today. One, I've got the best horse." She pointed to the first one in the number.

"Second, I've had the best trainer." She pointed to the second one. "And last of all," she pointed to the last one, "I'm a better rider than you."

"That depends on the judge, doesn't it?" Melody said. She started to walk away.

At that moment, an old battered Ford truck pulled into the fairgrounds. Hitched behind it was a rusty, two-horse trailer. Barely legible lettering on the side proclaimed, "Ace Farms. Quality Cutting Horses." The truck door opened, and a pretty dark-haired girl got out and ran to the table. She held several crumpled one-dollar bills in her hand.

"What's THAT?" Melody heard Jean say. "Who do they think they are by bringing something like THAT heap here?" Jean's voice carried. Her friends giggled.

The girl heard. Her face reddened, and she hurried back to the truck, holding tightly to number fifty-one. Melody glared at Jean. "You are so nasty," she said.

"Oh, oh. Melody's going to sing us a song," Jean chanted. "She's going to tell me I'm doing wrong." The other girls giggled again. Melody walked away.

On her way back to the trailer, Melody passed the dilapidated truck and trailer in time to see an elderly man standing by the ramp. A pretty little bay filly was backed out. Melody stopped to watch. The horse had the most delicate head she had ever seen. Her large eyes were set wide apart with a little star hung between them. The coat was a deep mahogany red, trimmed with black mane, tail and legs. Extra large ears made her look a little like a jackrabbit.

The girl glanced up at Melody and quickly looked away.

"That's a really cute horse you have there," Melody said. "What class are you in?"

"Green Horse," the girl said.

"Me, too. I hope you do well."

"Thanks," the girl mumbled, but she didn't look around.

Melody walked on. *She probably thinks I was part of Jean's group,* she thought sadly.

Mrs. Morrison and Abby were brushing Dancer's already gleaming coat. The filly was trying to reach the green grass at her feet, but the lead rope was tied too short.

"She's as bad as Miss Piggy," Melody laughed. She picked up a mane and tail comb and began smoothing out the long red tail. "I ran into Jean Monroe up there," she said. "She was being her usual witchy self."

"What'd she say?" her mother asked.

"It wasn't so much what she said to me, it was the way she acted when that old truck over there," Melody pointed one row over, "pulled in. It was as if you don't have a nice enough rig, you have no right to come here."

"Her grandfather Clarkston built the pavilion," Abby said. "Maybe she feels that gives her the right to think that way."

"It's still wrong," Melody said. "I felt so sorry for that poor girl. She's got the cutest little horse. You know, I hope she does well."

"Do you know which class she's in?" Abby asked.

"She said Green Horse."

"Wishing your competition good luck?" her mother teased.

"Maybe she'll beat out Jean."

"Maybe you will."

"I'm not counting on it. Say, where's the hair spray? This mane won't stay down."

After using half a bottle of the strongest holding hair spray she had been able to find, Melody finally got the stray section of mane to lie flat. "There, now stay," she told the stubborn hair. She watched for a moment. It didn't spring back up. She put the bottle in the tack box.

"It's time to get you ready," Abby said. "Here, let me pin the number on your shirt."

"Mom, have you seen Dad, yet?"

Mrs. Morrison shook her head. "You know how Seattle traffic can be."

Melody nodded. She stood still while Abby pinned her number on the back of the new western shirt Mom bought her only yesterday. Mrs. Morrison fussed with Melody's hair, tucking in stray wisps here and applying spray there. It was almost time. Her stomach churned. While she had been thinking about Jean's rudeness, she forgot to be nervous. But now there was nothing to take her mind off the upcoming event. Time had come for her to mount up and ride into her first class ever. She hoped her dad would make it on time.

CHAPTER THIRTEEN: GREEN HORSE CLASS

Melody wiped her hand against the leg of her jeans. "Lord, help me do good," she quietly prayed. The butterflies in her stomach were still agitated, and she was glad she didn't eat that sandwich her mother tried to press on her.

If Dancer was aware of her rider's jitters, she didn't show it. The red dun filly stood by the arena gate as though she had been through this routine many times before. The horse's liquid brown eyes took in the activity going on around her and in the ring. Her ears moved back and forth as different sounds caught her attention.

A stray wisp of mane broke loose and popped up. Melody pushed it down; it wouldn't stay. She tried wetting her finger to reactivate the hair spray, but all she succeeded in doing was cause another strand to break loose and pop up. There was no time for either Abby or her mother to get the bottle of hair spray from the truck.

"Class fifty-three, Green Horse," the loudspeaker blared. "Prepare to enter the ring."

Melody looked at the seats lining the sides of the pavilion. Her father wasn't among the spectators. He's not going to make it, Melody thought. He probably doesn't really care anyway. He didn't want me buying Dancer in the first place. She tightened her hold on the reins and tried to make it look as though she was a show veteran like most of those around her obviously were. A green rider on a green horse, she thought. What do I think I'm doing? Why did I ever let Mom and Abby talk me into this?

"You'll do just fine," her mother said, lightly touching Melody's arm. Off to one side, Abby gave a thumb's up sign and grinned, exposing a gap between her teeth.

Melody smiled wanly. She turned Dancer to follow the third horse, a sorrel gelding, into the arena. She felt the judge's eyes as Dancer walked steadily, smoothly, her head held at just the right height and angle.

There were seven horses total, all under five years old and all in their first year of training under a saddle. Jean was first in line on her gray Arabian gelding. The triple one's pinned on her shirt reminded Melody of the blond girl's boasting before the show.

"I hope we show her," Melody whispered. Dancer's ears flicked back to catch the words, and ever so slightly she nodded her head as if she agreed.

Melody didn't know who the older woman directly in front of her was, only that she was supposed to be a trainer of some kind. While waiting at the gate, Melody caught a glimpse of blood specks at the corner of her sorrel's mouth. She wasn't sure, but she thought she saw a twisted wire bit. From what she remembered reading in the rules book, harsh training devices weren't allowed in a green horse class.

Behind Dancer two more trainers were riding, followed by two horses mounted by out-of-valley contestants. One of those was the pretty dark-haired girl on the little bay filly. Melody felt anger all over again as she recalled how Jean and the others laughed behind their hands when the beat-up truck and trailer drove in. Melody saw the girl gripping the reins with whitened knuckles while they waited at the gate. Melody tried smiling at her, but the girl avoided looking in her direction. Melody hoped the little bay horse would do well for her rider.

The horses walked around the perimeter of the ring. Dancer kept her head down in perfect western pleasure form and moved smoothly, calmly. At the head of the procession, Jean's Arabian fought the bit and tossed its head. Several times Jean had to circle out into the ring to bring him under control. *It must be frustrating to have your horse act up like that,* Melody thought. *It serves her right for the way she treated me and that other girl, though.*

"Turn your horses and jog," the announcer ordered.

Each rider turned her horse toward the center of the arena and reversed direction. They urged their mounts into the slow, easy western trot that could cover a lot of distance in a day's time. Melody settled into the saddle and let her body move rhythmically with Dancer's motion.

One horse passed her, then another, but Dancer kept at the same steady pace. The horse ahead slowed to a walk. To avoid a collision, Melody guided Dancer into the center of the ring in order to pass. Dancer slowed. Melody pressed her legs against the red dun's sides. This was no time for Dancer to stop jogging. The command to walk hadn't been given yet.

Reluctantly, Dancer jogged another few feet; but she was tired for this had been a long day for a young horse. Besides, going around and around this arena was boring. She slowed to a walk. Melody glanced around. The judge's back was toward them. With both feet at the same time, Melody kicked Dancer hard in the ribs. The horse gave a little buck and started jogging again. Melody heard giggles from the end seats. Out of the corner of her eye, she saw the judge turn their way and watch them ride past.

"Line up in the center," blared the speakers.

One by one, the riders turned their mounts to the middle of the ring and formed a semi-straight line facing the judge and the ring steward.

"Back your horses three paces and stop."

Shifting her weight as she had been taught and pulling back slightly on the reins, Melody backed Dancer the required three paces, stopped her and let her take a half step forward. She tried to look relaxed as she again searched the stands for sight of her father. He was no where to be seen.

Melody watched the judge walk over to the sixth horse in line and say something to the rider. The rider's expression tightened. She jerked her horse's head around and rode stiff-backed to the exit gate.

There was no time to wonder what happened. The judge walked to the rider next to Melody and laid a hand on the sorrel horse's lathered neck.

"You're using a twisted wire," the judge said. "Why?"

"I always use them when training horses," the rider said. Her horse fidgeted and the woman tightened the reins. The sorrel tossed its head, but that only caused the bit to cut deeper into the already raw corners of his mouth. Fresh blood showed.

"That's pretty severe equipment," the judge said in a low voice. Melody strained to hear the rest. "If you were doing your job right, you wouldn't need anything harsher than a snaffle. I'm disqualifying you."

"You can't do that!" the rider snapped, but the look in the judge's eyes stopped her from saying more.

"Read the rule book," the judge said. "'No harsh training devices shall be used in the green horse class.'"

The woman's face hardened, and Melody could feel the sparks from her eyes as she took her horse out of line and rode to the far gate.

The judge turned toward Melody and placed a hand on Dancer's neck, which was just as dry as when they entered the arena. The horse turned to sniff the woman's short curly hair and tried to nibble her hat.

Melody's stomach lurched.

The woman gently turned Dancer's nose away. "How old is this filly?"

"Almost three."

"How long has she been ridden?"

Melody did some quick figuring. "We did ground work last summer and fall," she said. "Then this spring we started her under saddle. I've been riding her since May."

"You've done a nice job; keep it up." The judge gave Dancer another pat on the neck and turned to the next rider in line.

The words rang in Melody's ears. Did that mean she and Dancer had a chance? The judge seemed to like them. But had she seen the slowing down to a walk in the arena and the double kick to the ribs?

The next few minutes seemed like an eternity as the judge went from one horse to the next, speaking a few words to each contestant. Some of the horses tried to break formation, requiring their riders to bring them back into line. Several times Jean had to take her gelding into the center of the arena and circle him around before bringing him back to his place. Melody wondered if the judge would count that against her. This was a green horse class; and, as much as she hated to admit it, Jean was doing a good job controlling the high-strung Arabian colt. Dancer, in the meantime, stood where she had been stopped and never moved out of line.

Returning to the center of the ring, the judge faced the riders. She wrote something on a slip of paper and handed it to the ring steward; then she picked up a microphone.

"I want to commend all of you for a job well done," she said to the five remaining riders. "You've done a nice job with these young horses."

Melody's hopes fell, but outwardly she held her smile. The judge apparently told the same thing to all the riders that she told Melody. She had only been trying to be nice.

" . . .disqualified for using harsh training devices," she heard the judge saying. "You won't have to resort to such tactics if you learn how to work with your horse and try to understand him. If someone wants you to use a device or method you think is harsh or wrong, seek another opinion. You want your horse to be a trustworthy companion, not a frightened half-ton combination of muscle, nerves and bone that obeys only because it fears you. That's a disaster waiting to happen." The judge stopped talking and signaled to the announcer in his booth.

The loudspeaker crackled. "For the green horse class, third place goes to number fifty-one, Clare Logan."

Melody watched the dark-haired girl on her little bay filly ride forward to accept the green ribbon. A scattering of applause followed her out of the arena. Melody smiled at her as she passed. "Good work," she said, and was rewarded with a bright smile in return.

"Second place, number one hundred eleven, Jean Monroe."

So, for all her boasting, Jean hadn't made first place after all. Right or wrong, Melody felt a sense of satisfaction. It helped take away much of the hurt Jean's meanness caused her over the past several months.

"And first place goes to number eighty-seven . . ."

Melody's jaw dropped. That was her number. *But that isn't possible*, she protested inwardly. *This isn't really happening. Things like this happen only in movies and books.*

" . . .Melody Morrison."

"Way to go, Mel!" she heard Abby shout.

There was laughter, but friendly laughter this time, from the section where Jean's friends sat. Maybe it wasn't a dream after all. Maybe it really was happening. As Melody nudged Dancer forward to accept the coveted blue rosette and ribbon, she saw her father in the stands. She had never seen him look so proud.

CHAPTER FOURTEEN: GIFTS

After the show, Jean's mockery of Melody lost its effectiveness; and many of the other girls no longer followed her lead. Several of them began seeking Melody out between classes and talking with her. Soon Jean gave up, and Melody was able to attend school without fearing continual harassment.

Mick accompanied Melody as she delivered papers six days a week. On Saturdays when they went out to the ranch, he loved becoming a smelly, muddy mess by finding every fresh cow dropping he could and rolling in it. Afterwards he would run up to Melody and beg to be petted. He usually got a cold washing with the garden hose instead.

Melody's service to her paper customers was so appreciated that the tips she received during the monthly collecting enabled her to make an extra payment on Dancer the end of October.

Early in December, Melody sat at the kitchen table going over her paper route list and figuring out what she made the previous month. Her eyes grew wide when she wrote down the final figure. To make sure, she went over everything again. "Hey, Mom, guess what?"

Mrs. Morrison looked up from the shirt she was cutting out. "What?"

"With that extra payment, and with what I should be able to save from now until Christmas, I'll be able to pay off Dancer by the end of this month. Then she'll be all mine! Just think! My very own horse!"

"I'm very proud of you," her mother said. "And it wasn't just any old horse, either. It was the one you wanted."

"Dad, did you ever think I could do it?"

"Uh, what?" Her father turned from the computer. "Did I think you could do what?"

"Oh, Dad! I was talking about paying off Dancer by the end of December. Did you think I'd ever be able to do it? And two months early."

Her father took off his glasses and wiped them on the front of his shirt. "I guess I didn't think you'd stick with it," he said slowly, measuring his words. "You know I was opposed to it at the beginning; but I have to admit, you proved me wrong. I'm really proud of you."

Melody beamed. Praise from her dad came so seldom. It felt good.

December darkness had fallen when Melody delivered her last paper for the day two weeks before Christmas. She slung the empty canvas sack over her shoulder and, with Mick by her side, detoured to the little grocery store that served their tiny town.

"Sit," she commanded. He sat. "Stay." He remained in place while she went into the store.

There were a few more customers than usual, so Melody's purchase of ice cream for a family treat took longer than she expected. She was about to pay for it when she heard Mick barking and growling. Leaving the ice cream on the counter, Melody rushed out of the store in time to see a tall, thin man in a dirty plaid jacket drag Mick toward a muddy white pickup truck.

"Let go of my dog!" she yelled, rushing toward the man.

"Ain't your dog," the man said. He shoved Melody back. She stumbled backwards and sat hard on the sidewalk.

"He is too my dog! Abby gave him to me." Melody scrambled to her feet.

"Ain't her dog either. I paid good money for him."

This had to be the Mr. Lyton Abby sold Mick to over a year ago.

"But he ran away from you. He'd be dead if I didn't find him."

"Don't make no difference." The man grabbed Mick by the scruff of his neck and tossed him into the back of the truck. He slammed the canopy hatch and turned the handle. Mick barked and scratched the inside. Mr. Lyton walked to the cab of the truck.

"Wait!" Melody cried. "How much did you pay for him?"

"More 'en you got." The man got into the cab.

Melody grabbed the door to keep him from closing it. "How much?" she demanded.

"Two fifty." He tried to jerk the door out of her grip, but she held tight.

"Two hundred and fifty dollars?"

"Yep."

"I've got two hundred," Melody said, "and I'll have the other fifty in two weeks. You don't really want Mick back. He won't work sheep or cows any more." She knew that was a lie since Mick began working cattle after the wild dog attack, but she didn't want Mick going back to this man.

Mr. Lyton stroked his scraggly beard. "Give me the two hundred," he said, "and he's yours."

"It's at my house. If you follow me, we can go get it."

"Git in. I'll drive."

"No," Melody said. "I'll walk. It's only a few blocks."

"Have it your way." Mr. Lyton closed the truck door and started the engine.

Melody raced home, making sure the white truck followed her. Mick had fallen quiet, but she could see his eyes watching her through the canopy's window.

Rushing into the house, she let the door slam behind her. "Mom!" she called. "Come here, quick!"

Mrs. Morrison hurried from the kitchen, holding a wooden spoon dripping with batter.

"There's a man outside who said he's the one who bought Mick from Abby and he's going to take him but he'll let me buy him back for two hundred and I've got that much saved toward paying off Dancer and . . ." Melody had to stop to catch her breath.

"Whoa," her mother said. "Slow down. Who is this man? And where is Mick?"

"He put Mick in the back of his truck. He's outside. I told him to follow me home and I'd get the money to buy Mick back."

"Before you go handing over any money, let's make sure this man is on the up and up," Melody's father said, coming in from the garage in time to hear what was going on. "What's his name."

"Mr. Lyton."

"Okay," he said, "I'll go out and talk with him. Jen, you call Abby and verify what this man says is true. Melody, you stay in here with your mother."

"I'm going upstairs to get the money," Melody said when her father went out. Mrs. Morrison nodded. She had already dialed Abby's number and was listening to the phone ring at the other end.

"Abby verifies that Mr. Lyton did pay two hundred fifty for Mick," Melody heard her mother tell her father. "Since the dog was considered lost through no fault of hers when he told her he had run off, she didn't contact him nor offer to give his money back when Mick showed up last fall."

"And his identification shows he is who he says he is," her father replied. "Jen, write up a receipt for that man to sign. He's agreed to turn over all rights to Mick for the two hundred, and I want to be sure he keeps his word."

Melody walked into the kitchen, a packet of neatly folded ones, fives, and tens in her hand. "Here's the money," she said and handed it to her father.

Mr. Morrison counted out the bills while his wife wrote up the receipt. Again, he told Melody to stay in the house while he went outside. The minutes dragged. Melody wanted to look out the window, but her mother held her back. More time elapsed. What was taking them so long?

The front door opened. Melody heard the truck drive away. A forty-five pound black-and-white wiggling body threw itself against her. "Mick!" she cried, falling back into the sofa. He was all over her, licking her face, her hands, any part of her he could reach. "Thanks, Dad."

"I'd never pay that kind of money for a dog," he said, "but I guess you think he's worth it."

"Yes, he's worth it. Even if I have to wait a month longer for Dancer to be all mine, he's worth it."

Shaking his head, Mr. Morrison retreated to his study. "You and your animals," he muttered. Melody and her mother looked at each other and smiled.

On Christmas Eve the papers arrived at Melody's house before noon. She looked forward to getting done early and having time to wrap the gifts she bought her brothers and parents. Both Randy and Jeff were coming from Seattle in the morning. Abby was going to join them for Christmas Eve dinner. Melody had already wrapped Abby's gift, something she made in art class.

Elderly Mrs. Nenana met Melody at the door. "Here's a little something for you, child," she said, and she handed the girl a small gold-wrapped box and a card. "Merry Christmas."

"Thank you," Melody said, handing her the paper as she took the gift. "And merry Christmas to you, too." She tucked the box and card into her canvas paper pouch.

A good half of Melody's customers were waiting for her and opened their doors when she approached their houses with the paper. From some, there was a card and a small wrapped gift. Many gave home-baked cookies, and others gave cards only. Melody's bag didn't lighten as it usually did . When the route took her near home, she stopped and unloaded the collection of gifts on the kitchen table.

It was almost dark by the time Melody finished her deliveries. The time saved by receiving her papers early had been used up by the many Christmas wishes and gifts. Some of the customers even remembered Mick; he received gift boxes of dog biscuits, a bright red collar, and a squeaky toy in the shape of a hot dog.

"Mom, can you believe all this stuff?" Melody asked. She sat at the table and opened one of the cards. A ten dollar bill dropped out with a note that expressed gratitude for the good job she had done over the past year.

Melody opened card after card. Most held one or two dollars, others held a five or a ten. And one card had a neatly folded twenty dollar bill in it.

"Mom, these people didn't have to do this," Melody said.

"No," her mother replied. "They didn't have to do it. They wanted to do it. Just like you didn't have to go out of your way as much as you did for them. You did it because you wanted to. People appreciate that. This is their way of thanking you."

"I guess so. I wonder how much is here."

"Well, count it."

Melody counted the bills on the table. She shook her head. Again, she counted them, and the total came out the same.

"There's a hundred and thirty-two dollars here," she said. "Almost what I need to pay Dancer off two months early."

"Maybe this will help." Mr. Morrison came into the kitchen and handed Melody an envelope. She took it, a puzzled look on her face. "Well, open it," he said.

Melody tore it open. A crisp fifty dollar bill dropped out. "Oh, Dad! Thank you!" She threw her arms around his neck. "Now I can pay Dancer off early. I can do it tonight when Abby comes."

"Which means you better get the table cleared and set for dinner," Mrs. Morrison laughed. "She'll be here any moment."

Melody was placing the centerpiece on the table when she heard Abby's vehicle pull up in front of the house. She ran to the door and opened it before the bell rang. Abby was carrying a huge, brown box tied with several strands of different colored ribbons. She handed it to Melody, who nearly dropped it from the weight.

"What's in this?" Melody gasped, taking the box over to the tree and setting it on the floor. "It feels as heavy as one of your saddles."

"You'll find out in due time," Abby said. She and Mrs. Morrison shook their heads slightly when they exchanged glances.

Melody took an envelope off the table and handed it to Abby. "What's this?"

"The final payment on Dancer," Melody said. Her eyes shone. "You might say Dancer's my Christmas present to myself."

"Well you earned her," Abby said. "How did you manage this after paying Mr. Lyton for Mick?"

Melody and her mother told her about the generous gifts from the paper customers and her father's surprise gift.

"You're a hard worker, girl," Abby said. "With the good attitude you've got, you'll go far."

Dinner was a cheerful affair. Mr. Morrison joined in conversation more than Melody ever remembering him doing. Mrs. Morrison had cooked a wonderful turkey with stuffing, gravy, mashed potatoes, salads, and homemade rolls. Afterwards, they gathered in the living room with mugs of fragrant hot cider. After her father read the Christmas story from the Bible, Melody gave her gift to Abby.

Abby opened the small, flat box and took out a ceramic tile mounted in a wooden frame. The title was a bas-relief rendition of a horse's head, which Melody glazed to resemble Dancer.

"Did you make this?" Abby asked.

Melody nodded. "We did those in art class this quarter. I wanted you to have it."

"It's really beautiful. And very special," Abby said. "I know just the place I'm going to hang it." With her toe, she nudged the box she brought. "Go ahead and open it."

Melody tried to untie the ribbons, but there were too many of them and they tangled. Her father took out a pocket knife and cut through them with one easy swipe. The flaps sprung open. Melody looked inside the box and gasped. "Oh, Abby, you shouldn't have!"

Abby's black show saddle, with all its silver trim brightly polished, lay in a nest of foam popcorn.

"You'll get more use out of it than I ever will," Abby said. "My husband would have wanted it this way." She leaned over and picked up a small gold-wrapped box off the floor. "Did you drop this?" she asked, handing it to Melody.

"I guess I did. It looks like the box Mrs. Nenana gave me."

Melody tore off the wrapping to reveal a small plush-covered jewelry case. She opened the lid. A golden horse head was set within a rhinestone studded horseshoe and hung on a delicate golden chain. Melody took the necklace out of the box and the pendant flipped over. There was something engraved on the back. Looking closer, Melody read the inscription. She began to laugh.

"I told Mrs. Nenana how I met Dancer," she explained to the puzzled expressions around her. "Look what she had engraved on the back." She handed the necklace to Abby.

Her parents crowded around to look at the pendant with Abby. All three had to squint in order to read the flowing script: "Love at first klonk."

A MESSAGE TO MY READERS

The story of Melody and Dancer is not entirely fiction. Many of the events experienced by them were actually lived by my thirteen-year-old daughter, Sheryl, and the young horse she fell in love with, DeeDee. The chapters about "whack," the contract, cow pies and green horse class are written pretty much as they actually took place. As I lived this story with my daughter, over and over I marveled how God helped all things to work together so she could realize her dream of owning a horse—not just any horse—DeeDee. Together, we both learned a lot about horses, and eventually I realized my own lifelong dream of owning a horse–but that's another story.

I'm a firm believer in prayer. Although God doesn't always answer the way I would like Him to, He does answer—and many times in ways far better than what I asked for. More importantly, He gives us the ability to live rightly in a world where so much ugliness is taking place. Life is not always easy for those who try to live righteously, who try to treat others with kindness and respect, who are willing to work hard and who are honest. But if we trust in Him and seek to obey Him, God rewards us with blessings too numerous to count.

I hope you will be encouraged by this story to dream your dreams and to trust God in helping you see them come true.

Bonnie Clement
April, 2000